PRAISE FOR PATRICIA HIGHSMITH

"She edges her readers toward the insane territory inhabited by her people. . . . Readers are sure to be left feeling by turns startled, oppressed, amused and queasy." —*New York Times Book Review*

"Savage in the way of Rabelais or Swift."
—Joyce Carol Oates, *New York Review of Books*

"Highsmith's gift as a suspense novelist is to show how this secret desire can bridge the normal and abnormal. . . . She seduces us with whisky-smooth surfaces only to lead us blindly into darker terrain." —*Commercial Appeal*

"Patricia Highsmith's novels are peerlessly disturbing . . . bad dreams that keep us thrashing for the rest of the night."
—*The New Yorker*

"A border zone of the macabre, the disturbing, the not quite accidental. . . . Highsmith achieves the effect of the occult without any recourse to supernatural machinery." —*New York Times Book Review*

"Though Highsmith would no doubt disclaim any kinship with Jonathan Swift or Evelyn Waugh, the best of [her work] is in the same tradition. . . . It is Highsmith's dark and sometimes savage humor and the intelligence that informs her precise and hard-edged prose which puts one in mind of those authors."
—*Newsday*

"Murder, in Patricia Highsmith's hands, is made to occur almost as casually as the bumping of a fender or a bout of food poisoning. This downplaying of the dramatic . . . has been much praised, as has the ordinariness of the details with which she depicts the daily lives and mental processes of her psychopaths. Both undoubtedly contribute to the domestication of crime in her fiction, thereby implicating the reader further in the sordid fantasy that is being worked out." —Robert Towers, *New York Review of Books*

"For eliciting the menace that lurks in familiar surroundings, there's no one like Patricia Highsmith." —*Time*

"The feeling of menace behind most Highsmith novels, the sense that ideas and attitudes alien to the reasonable everyday ordering of society are suggested, has made many readers uneasy. One closes most of her books with a feeling that the world is more dangerous than one had ever imagined." —Julian Symons, *New York Times Book Review*

"Mesmerizing . . . not to be recommended for the weak-minded and impressionable." —*Washington Post Book World*

"A writer who has created a world of her own—a world claustrophobic and irrational which we enter each time with a sense of personal danger. . . . Miss Highsmith is the poet of apprehension." —Graham Greene

"Patricia Highsmith is often called a mystery or crime writer, which is a bit like calling Picasso a draftsman." —*Cleveland Plain Dealer*

"An atmosphere of nameless dread, of unspeakable foreboding, permeates every page of Patricia Highsmith, and there's nothing quite like it." —*Boston Globe*

"[Highsmith] has an uncanny feeling for the rhythms of terror." —*Times Literary Supplement*

"To call Patricia Highsmith a thriller writer is true but not the whole truth: her books have stylistic texture, psychological depth, mesmeric readability." —*Sunday Times* (London)

"Highsmith is an exquisitely sardonic etcher of the casually treacherous personality." —*Newsday*

"Highsmith's novels skew your sense of literary justice, tilt your internal scales of right and wrong. The ethical order of things in the real world seems less stable [as she] deftly warps the moral sense of her readers." —*Cleveland Plain Dealer*

"Highsmith . . . conveys a firm, unshakable belief in the existence of evil—personal, psychological, and political. . . . The genius of Highsmith's writing is that it is at once deeply disturbing and exhilarating." —*Boston Phoenix*

"No one has created psychological suspense more densely and deliciously satisfying." —*Vogue*

"Read [*The Selected Stories*] at your own risk, knowing that this is not everyone's cup of poisoned tea." —Janet Maslin, *New York Times*

ALSO BY PATRICIA HIGHSMITH

Little Tales
of Misogyny

Patricia Highsmith

W. W. NORTON & COMPANY

NEW YORK LONDON

First published in German as *Kleine Geschichten für Weiberfeinde*
in a translation by W. E. Richartz.
Copyright © 1975 by Diogenes Verlag AG Zurich.

Original English text first published in Great Britain 1977.
Copyright © 1977 by Diogenes Verlag AG Zurich.

First published as a Norton paperback 2002

First published in Great Britain in 1977 by Heinemann
First published in the United States in 1986 by Penzler Books

For information about permission to reproduce selections from this book,
write to Permissions, W. W. Norton & Company, Inc., 500 Fifth Avenue,
New York, NY 10110

The text of this book is composed in Bembo
Design and composition by Amanda Morrison
Manufacturing by LSC Harrisonburg

Library of Congress Cataloging-in-Publication Data

Highsmith, Patricia, 1921–
    Little tales of misogyny / by Patricia Highsmith.
      p. cm.
    ISBN 0-393-32337-4 pbk.
    1. Women—Fiction. I. Title.

PS3558.I366 L5 2002
813'.54—dc21   2002016669

W. W. Norton & Company, Inc.
500 Fifth Avenue, New York, N.Y. 10110
www.wwnorton.com

W. W. Norton & Company Ltd.
15 Carlisle Street, London W1D 3BS

2 3 4 5 6 7 8 9 0

CONTENTS

Little Tales
of Misogyny

The Hand

A young man asked a father for his daughter's hand, and received it in a box—her left hand.

Father: "You asked for her hand and you have it. But it is my opinion that you wanted other things and took them."

Young man: "Whatever do you mean?"

Father: "Whatever do you think I mean? You cannot deny that I am more honorable than you, because you took something from my family without asking, whereas when you asked for my daughter's hand, I gave it."

Actually, the young man had not done anything dishonorable. The father was merely suspicious and had a dirty mind. The father could legally make the young man responsible for his daughter's upkeep and soak him financially. The young man could not deny that he had the daughter's hand—even though in desperation he had now buried it, after kissing it. But it was becoming two weeks old.

The young man wanted to see the daughter, and made an effort, but was quite blocked by besieging tradesmen. The daughter was signing checks with her right hand. Far from bleeding to death, she was going ahead at full speed.

The young man announced in newspapers that she had quit his bed and board. But he had to prove that she had ever enjoyed them. It was not yet "a marriage" on paper, or in the church. Yet there was no doubt that he had her hand, and had signed a receipt for it when the package had been delivered.

"Her hand in *what*?" the young man demanded of the police, in despair and down to his last penny. "Her hand is buried in my garden."

"You are a criminal to boot? Not merely disorganized in your way of life, but a psychopath? Did you by chance cut off your wife's hand?"

"I did not, and she is not even my wife!"

"He has her hand, and yet she is not his wife!" scoffed the men of the law. "What shall we do with him? He is unreasonable, maybe even insane."

"Lock him up in an asylum. He is also broke, so it will have to be a State Institution."

So the young man was locked up, and once a month the girl whose hand he had received came to look at him through the wire barrier, like a dutiful wife. And like most wives, she had nothing to say. But she smiled prettily. His job provided a small pension now, which she was getting. Her stump was concealed in a muff.

Because the young man became too disgusted with her to look at her, he was placed in a more disagreeable ward, deprived of books and company, and he went really insane.

When he became insane, all that had happened to him, the asking for and receiving his beloved's hand, became intelligible to him. He realized what a horrible mistake, crime even, he had been guilty of in demanding such a barbaric thing as a girl's hand.

He spoke to his captors, saying that now he understood his mistake.

"What mistake? To ask for a girl's hand? So did I, when I married."

The young man, feeling now he was insane beyond repair, since he could make contact with nothing, refused to eat for many days, and at last lay on his bed with his face to the wall, and died.

Oona, the Jolly Cave Woman

She was a bit hairy, one front tooth missing, but her sex appeal was apparent at a distance of two hundred yards or more, like an odor, which perhaps it was. She was round, round-bellied, round-shouldered, round-hipped, and always smiling, always jolly. That was why men liked her. She had always something cooking in a pot on a fire. She was simple-minded and never lost her temper. She had been clubbed over the head so many times, her brain was addled. It was not necessary to club Oona to have her, but that was the custom, and Oona barely troubled to dodge to protect herself.

Oona was constantly pregnant and had never experienced the onset of puberty, her father having had at her since she was five, and after him, her brothers. Her first child was born when she was seven. Even in late pregnancy she was interfered with, and men waited impatiently the half hour or so it took her to give birth before they fell on her again.

Oddly, she kept the birthrate of the tribe more or less steady, and if anything tended to decrease the population, since men neglected their own wives because of thinking of her, or occasionally were killed in fighting over her.

Oona was at last killed by a jealous woman whose husband had not touched her in many months. This man was the first to fall in love. His name was Vipo. His men-friends had laughed at him for not taking some other woman, or his own wife, in the times when Oona was not available. Vipo had lost an eye in fighting his rivals. He was only a middle-sized man. He had always brought Oona the choicest things he had killed. He worked long and hard to make an ornament out of flint, so he became the first artist of his tribe. All the others used flint only for arrowheads or knives. He had given the ornament to Oona to hang around her neck by a string of leather.

When Vipo's wife slew Oona out of jealousy, Vipo slew his wife in hatred and wrath. Then he sang a loud and tragic song. He continued to sing like a madman, as tears ran down his hairy cheeks. The tribe considered killing him, because he was mad and different from everyone else, and they were afraid. Vipo drew images of Oona in the wet sand by the sea, then pictures of her on the flat stones on the mountains near by, pictures that could be seen from a distance. He made a statue of Oona out of wood, then one of stone. Sometimes he slept with these. Out of the clumsy syllables of his language, he made a sentence which evoked Oona whenever he uttered it. He was not the only one who learned and uttered this sentence, or who had known Oona.

Vipo was slain by a jealous woman whose man had not touched her for months. Her man had purchased one of Vipo's statues of Oona for a great price—a vast piece of leather made of several bison hides. Vipo made a beautiful watertight house of it, and had enough left over for clothing for himself. He created more sentences about Oona. Some men had admired him, others had hated him, and all the women had hated him because he had looked at them as if he did not see them. Many men were sad when Vipo was dead.

But in general people were relieved when Vipo was gone. He had been a strange one, disturbing some people's sleep at night.

The Coquette

There was once a coquette who had a suitor whom she couldn't get rid of. He took her promises and avowals seriously, and would not leave. He even believed her hints. This annoyed her, because it got in the way of new temporary acquaintances, their presents, flattery, flowers, dinners and so forth.

Finally Yvonne insulted and lied to her suitor Bertrand, and gave him literally nothing—which was a minus compared to the nothing she was giving her other men-friends. Still Bertrand would not cease his attentions, because he considered her behavior normal and feminine, an excess of modesty. She even gave him a lecture, and for once in her life she told the truth. Unaccustomed as he was to the truth, expecting falsehood from a pretty woman, he took her words as turnabouts, and continued to dance attendance.

Yvonne attempted to poison him by means of arsenic in cups of chocolate at her house, but he recovered and thought this a greater and more charming proof of her fear of losing her virginity with him, though she had already lost her virginity at the age of ten, when she had told her mother that she was raped. Yvonne had thus sent a thirty-year-old man to prison. She had been trying for two weeks to seduce him, saying she was fifteen, and mad about him. It had given her pleasure to ruin his career and to make his wife unhappy and ashamed, and their eight-year-old daughter bewildered.

Other men gave Bertrand advice. "We have all had it," they said, "maybe even been to bed with her once or twice. You haven't even had that. And she's worthless!" But Bertrand thought he was different in Yvonne's eyes, and though he realized he had pertinacity beyond the common order, he felt this a virtue.

Yvonne incited a new suitor to kill Bertrand. She won the new suitor's allegiance by promising to marry him, if he eliminated Bertrand. To Bertrand, she said the same thing about the other man. The new suitor challenged Bertrand to a duel, missed the first shot, and then began talking with his intended victim. (Bertrand's gun had refused to fire at all.) They discovered that each had been given promises of marriage. Meanwhile both men had given her expensive presents and had lent her money during small crises over the past months.

They were resentful, but could not come up with an idea for scotching her. So they decided to kill her. The new suitor went to her and told her he had killed the stupid and persistent Bertrand. Then Bertrand knocked on the door. The two men pretended to fight each other. In reality, they pushed Yvonne between them and killed her with various blows about the head. Their story was that she tried to interfere and was accidentally struck.

Since the judge of the town had himself suffered and been laughed at by the townsfolk because of Yvonne's coquetry with him, he was secretly pleased by her death, and let the two men off without ado. He was also wise enough to know that the two men could not have killed her if they had not been infatuated with her—a state that inspired his pity, since he had become sixty years old.

Only Yvonne's maid, who had always been well paid and tipped, attended her funeral. Even Yvonne's family detested her.

The Female Novelist

She has total recall. It is all sex. She is on her third marriage now, having dropped three children on the way, but none by her present husband. Her cry is: "Listen to my past! It is more important than my present. Let me tell you what an absolute swine my last husband (or lover) was."

Her past is like an undigested, perhaps indigestible meal which sits upon her stomach. One wishes she could simply vomit and forget it.

She writes reams about how many times she, or her woman rival, jumped into bed with her husband. And how she paced the floor, sleepless—virtuously denying herself the consolation of a drink—while her husband spent the night with the other woman, flagrantly, etc., and to hell with what friends and neighbors thought. Since the friends and neighbors were either incapable of thinking or were uninterested in the situation, it doesn't matter what they thought. One might say that this is the time for a novelist's invention, for creating thought and public opinion where there is none, but the female novelist doesn't bother inventing. It is all stark as a jockstrap.

After three women-friends have seen and praised the manuscript, saying it is "just like life," and the male and female characters' names have been changed four times, much to the detriment of the manuscript's appearance, and after one man-friend (a prospective lover) has read the first page and returned the manuscript saying he has read it all and adores it—the manuscript goes off to a publisher. There is a quick, courteous rejection.

She begins to be more cautious, secures entrées via writer acquaintances, vague, hedged-about recommendations obtained at the expense of winy lunches and dinners.

Rejection after rejection, nonetheless.

"I *know* my story is important!" she says to her husband.

"So is the life of the mouse here, to him—or maybe her," he replies. He is a patient man, but nearly at the end of his nerves with all this.

"What mouse?"

"I talk to a mouse nearly every morning when I'm in the bathtub. I think his or her problem is food. They're a pair. Either one or the other comes out of the hole—there's a hole in the corner of the bathroom—then I get them something from the refrigerator."

"You're wandering. What's that got to do with my manuscript?"

"Just that mice are concerned with a more important subject—food. Not with whether your ex-husband was unfaithful to you, or whether you suffered from it, even in a setting as beautiful as Capri or Rapallo. Which gives me an idea."

"What?" she asks, somewhat anxiously.

Her husband smiles for the first time in several months. He experiences a few seconds of peace. There is not the clicking of the typewriter in the house. His wife is actually looking at him, waiting to hear what he has to say. "You figure that one out. You're the one with imagination. I won't be in for dinner."

Then he leaves the flat, taking his address book and—optimistically—a pair of pajamas and a toothbrush.

She goes and stares at the typewriter, thinking that perhaps here is another novel, just from this evening, and should she scrap the novel she has fussed over for so long and start this new one? Maybe tonight? Now? Who is he going to sleep with?

The Dancer

They danced marvelously together, swooping back and forth across the floor to the erotic rhythms of the tango, sometimes the waltz. At the age of twenty and twenty-two respectively, Claudette and Rodolphe became lovers. They wanted to marry, but their employer thought they were more titillating to the customers if they were not married. So they remained single.

The nightclub where they worked was called The Rendez-vous, and was known amongst a certain jaded, middle-aged male clientele as a sure cure for impotence. Just come and watch Claudette and Rodolphe dance, everyone said. Journalists, trying to spice their columns, described their act as sado-masochistic, because Rodolphe often appeared to be choking Claudette to death. He would seize her throat and advance, bending her backward, or he would retreat—it didn't matter—keeping her throat in the grip of his hands, sometimes shaking her neck so that her hair tossed wildly. The audience would gasp, sigh, and watch with fascination. The drumrolls of the three-man band would grow louder and more insistent.

Claudette stopped sleeping with Rodolphe, because she thought deprivation would whet his appetite. It was easy for Claudette to excite Rodolphe when dancing with him, then to abandon him with a flounce as she made her exit to the applause, sometimes the laughter, of the spectators. Little did they know that Rodolphe was really being abandoned.

Claudette was whimsical, with no real plans, but she took up with a paunchy man called Charles, good-natured, generous and rich. She even slept with him. Charles applauded loudly when Claudette and Rodolphe danced together, Rodolphe with his hands about Claudette's graceful white neck, and she bending backward. Charles could afford to laugh. He was going to bed with her later.

Since their earnings were bound together, Rodolphe put it up to Claudette: stop seeing Charles, or he would not perform with her. Or at least he would not perform with his hands about her throat as if he were going to throttle her in an excess of passion, which was what the customers came for. Rodolphe meant it, so Claudette promised not to sleep with Charles again. She kept her promise, Charles drifted away and was seen at The Rendez-vous seldom, and then sadly moping, and finally he stopped coming at all. But Rodolphe gradually realized that Claudette was taking on two or three other men. She began sleeping with these, and business went up more than it had with the rich Charles, who after all was only one man, with one group of friends whom he could bring to The Rendez-vous.

Rodolphe asked Claudette to drop all three. She promised. But either they or their messengers with notes and flowers still hung around the dressing room every evening.

Rodolphe, who had not spent a night with Claudette in five months now, yet whose body was pressed against hers every night before the eyes of two hundred people—Rodolphe danced a splendid tango one evening. He pressed himself against her as usual, and she bent backward.

"More! More!" cried the audience, mostly men, as Rodolphe's hands tightened about her throat.

Claudette always pretended to suffer, to love Rodolphe and to suffer at the hands of his passion in the dance. This time she did not rise when he released her. Nor did he assist her, as he usually did. He had strangled her, too tightly for her to cry out. Rodolphe walked off the little stage, and left Claudette for other people to pick up.

The Invalid, or,
the Bedridden

She had suffered a fall while on a skiing holiday at Chamonix with her boyfriend some ten years ago. The injury had something to do with her back. The doctors couldn't find anything, nobody could see anything wrong with her back, but still it hurt, she said. Actually, she was not sure she would get her man unless she pretended an injury, and one acquired when she had been with him. Philippe, however, was quite in love with her, and she need not have worried so much. Still, hooking Philippe very firmly, plus ensuring a life of leisure—not to say flat on her back in bed, or however she chose to lie comfortably, for the rest of her life—was no small gain. It was a big one. How many other women could capture a man for life, give him nothing at all, not even bother to cook his meals, and still be supported in rather fine style?

Some days she got up, mainly out of boredom. She was sometimes up when the sun was shining, but not always. When the sun was not shining, or when there was a threat of rain, Christine felt terrible and kept to her bed. Then her husband Philippe had to go downstairs with the shopping net and come back and cook. All Christine talked about was "how I feel." Visitors and friends were treated to a long account of injections, pills, pains in the back which had kept her from sleeping last Wednesday night, and the possibility of rain tomorrow, because of the way she felt.

But she was always feeling rather well when August came, because she and Philippe went to Cannes then. Things might be bad at the very start of August, however, causing Philippe to engage an ambulance to Orly, then a special accommodation on an aeroplane to Nice. In Cannes she found herself able to go to the beach every morning at 11 A.M., swimming for a few minutes with the aid of water wings, and to eat a good lunch. But at the end of August, back in Paris, she suffered a relapse from all the excitement, rich food, and general physical strain, and once more had to take to bed, her tan included. She would sometimes expose tanned legs for visitors, sigh with memories of Cannes, then cover up again with sheets and blanket. September heralded, indeed, the onset of grim winter. Philippe couldn't sleep with her now—though for God's sake he felt he had earned better treatment, having worked his fingers to the bone to pay her doctors', radiologists' and pharmacies' bills beyond reckoning. He would have to face another solitary winter, and not even in the same room with her, but in the next room.

"To think I brought all this upon her," Philippe said to one of his friends, "by taking her to Chamonix."

"But why is she always feeling quite well in August?" replied the friend. "You think she is an invalid? Think again, really, old man."

Philippe did begin to think, because other friends had said the same thing. It took him years to think, many years of Augusts in Cannes (at an expense which knocked out the savings of a whole eleven months) and many winters sleeping mainly in the "spare bedroom," and not with the woman he loved and desired.

So the eleventh August in Cannes, Philippe summoned all his courage. He swam out behind Christine with a pin in his fingers. He stuck a pin in her water wings and made two punctures, one in each white wing. He and Christine were not far out, just slightly over their heads in water. Philippe was not in the best of form. Not only was he losing his hair, of no importance in a swimming situation, but he had developed a belly, which might not, he thought, have come if he had been able to make love to Christine all the past decade. But Philippe tried and succeeded in pushing Christine under, and at the same time had some difficulty in keeping himself afloat. His confused motions, seen by a few people finally, appeared to be those of a man trying to save someone who was drowning. And this of course was what he told the police and everyone. Christine, despite sufficient buoyant fat, sank like a piece of lead.

Christine was absolutely no loss to Philippe except for burial fees. He soon lost his paunch, and much to his own surprise found himself suddenly well-to-do, instead of having to turn every penny. His friends congratulated him, but politely, and in the abstract. They couldn't exactly say, "Thank God, you're rid of that bitch," but they said the next thing to it. In about six months, he met quite a nice girl who loved to cook, was full of energy, and she also liked to go to bed with him. The hair on Philippe's head even began to grow back.

The Artist

At the time Jane got married, one would have thought there was nothing unusual about her. She was plump, pretty and practical: she could give artificial respiration at the drop of a hat or pull someone out of a faint or a nosebleed. She was a dentist's assistant, and as cool as they come in the face of crisis or pain. But she had enthusiasm for the arts. What arts? All of them. She began, in the first year of her married life, with painting. This occupied all her Saturdays, or enough of Saturdays to prevent adequate shopping for the weekend, but her husband Bob did the shopping. He also paid for the framing of muddy, run-together oil portraits of their friends, and the sittings of the friends took up time on the weekends too. Jane at last faced the fact she could not stop her colors from running together, and decided to abandon painting for the dance.

The dance, in a black leotard, did not much improve her robust figure, only her appetite. Special shoes followed. She was studying ballet. She had discovered an institution called The School of Arts. In this five-story edifice they taught the piano, violin and other instruments, music composition, novel writing, poetry, sculpture, the dance and painting.

"You see, Bob, life can and should be made more beautiful," Jane said with her big smile. "And everyone wants to contribute, if he or she can, just a little bit to the beauty and poetry of the world."

Meanwhile, Bob emptied the garbage and made sure they were not out of potatoes. Jane's ballet did not progress beyond a certain point, and she dropped it and took up singing.

"I really think life is beautiful enough as it is," Bob said. "Anyway I'm pretty happy." That was during Jane's singing period, which had caused them to crowd the already small living room with an upright piano.

For some reason, Jane stopped her singing lessons and began to study sculpture and wood carving. This made the living room a mess of dropped bits of clay and wood chips which the vacuum could not always pick up. Jane was too tired for anything after her day's work in the dentist's office, and standing on her feet over wood or clay until midnight.

Bob came to hate The School of Arts. He had seen it a few times, when he had gone to fetch Jane at 11 P.M. or so. (The neighborhood was dangerous to walk in.) It seemed to Bob that the students were all a lot of misguided hopefuls, and the teachers a lot of mediocrities. It seemed a madhouse of misplaced effort. And how many homes, children and husbands were being troubled now, because the women of the households—the students were mainly women—were not at home performing a few essential tasks? It seemed to Bob that there was no inspiration in The School of Arts, only a desire to imitate people who had been inspired, like Chopin, Beethoven and Bach, whose works he could hear being mangled as he sat on a bench in the lobby, awaiting his wife. People called artists mad, but these students seemed incapable of the same kind of madness. The students did appear insane, in a certain sense of the word, but not in the right way, somehow. Considering the time The School of Arts deprived him of his wife, Bob was ready to blow the whole building to bits.

He had not long to wait, but he did not blow the building up himself. Someone—it was later proven to have been an instructor— put a bomb under The School of Arts, set to go off at 4 P.M. It was New Year's Eve, and despite the fact it was a semi-holiday, the students of all the arts were practicing diligently. The police and some newspapers had been forewarned of the bomb. The trouble was, nobody found it, and also most people did not believe that any bomb would go off. Because of the seediness of the neighborhood, the school had been subjected to scares and threats before. But the bomb went off, evidently from the depths of the basement, and a pretty good-sized one it was.

Bob happened to be there, because he was to have fetched Jane at 5 P.M. He had heard about the bomb rumor, but did not know whether to believe it or not. With some caution, however, or a premonition, he was waiting across the street instead of in the lobby.

One piano went through the roof, a bit separated from the student who was still seated on the stool, fingering nothing. A dancer at last made a few complete revolutions without her feet touching the ground, because she was a quarter of a mile high, and her toes were even pointing skyward. An art student was flung through a wall, his brush poised, ready to make the master stroke as he floated horizontally towards a true oblivion. One instructor, who had taken refuge as often as possible in the toilets of The School of Arts, was blown up in proximity to some of the plumbing.

Then came Jane, flying through the air with a mallet in one hand, a chisel in the other, and her expression was rapt. Was she stunned, still concentrating on her work, or even dead? Bob could not tell about Jane. The flying particles subsided with a gentle, diminishing clatter, and a rise of gray dust. There were a few seconds of silence, during which Bob stood still. Then he turned and walked homeward. Other schools of art, he knew, would arise. Oddly, this thought crossed his mind before he realized that his wife was gone forever.

The Middle-Class Housewife

Pamela Thorpe considered Women's Lib one of those silly protest movements that journalists liked to write about to fill their pages. Women's Lib claimed to want "independence" for women, whereas Pamela believed that women had the upper hand over men anyway. So what was all the fuss about?

The reason this question arose at all was because Pamela's daughter Barbara came home in June after graduating from university, and told her mother that there was going to be a Women's Lib rally in their neighborhood. Barbara had organized it with her college chum Fran, whose family Pamela knew. Of course Pamela went to the rally—in the local church—mainly to amuse herself and to hear what the younger generation had to say.

Colored balloons and paper streamers hung from the rafters and the sills of stained glass windows. Pamela was surprised to see young Connie Haines, mother of two small children, preaching away like a convert.

"Working women need *free state nurseries!*" shouted Connie, and her last words were almost obliterated by applause. "And *alimony*—the legalized soaking of divorced husbands—must *go!*"

Cheers! Women got to their feet clapping and shouting.

State nurseries! Pamela envisaged streams of working women (they only thought they wanted to work) abandoning their homes at 8 A.M., parking their tots somewhere, bringing home paychecks at the end of the week to houses where the next meal wasn't even on the stove. Many women were now raising their hands to be given the floor, so Pamela raised her hand, too. There was a lot she wanted to say.

"*Men* are not against us!" one woman cried out from a pew. "It is *women* who hold us back, selfish, cowardly women who think they'll be losing something by demanding equal pay for equal work! . . ."

"My *husband,*" Connie began, because she suddenly had the floor again, and was speaking in an even louder voice, "is about to take his final exams to become a doctor, and we're worried because we can hardly make ends meet. I've got to stay home and look after the two kids. If we hired a baby-sitter, it would cancel out my earnings if I took a job! *That's* why I'm in favor of free state nurseries! I'm not too lazy to take a job!"

More applause and cheering.

Now Pamela got to her feet. "State nurseries!" she said, and she had to be heard, because her voice overrode all the others. "You younger people—I'm forty-two—seem not to realize that a woman's place is in the home, to make a home, that you'll be breeding a generation of delinquents if a generation of state nursery–raised children—"

A general uproar silenced Pamela for a moment.

"That has not been proven!" a girl's voice yelled.

"And abolition of alimony! Maybe you're against that, too?" someone else demanded. It was her daughter Barbara.

The faces had become a blur. Pamela recognized some of them, neighbors since years, but in a way she couldn't recognize them in their new roles of attackers, enemies. "As for alimony," Pamela resumed, still on her feet, "it is a husband's *job* to support the family, is it not?"

"Even when a wife has walked out?" asked someone.

"Do you know some women are getting away with murder, and it's giving women a bad name?"

"Every divorce case should be examined *separately!*" cried another voice.

"Women will be victimized!" Pamela shot back. "The abolition of alimony has been called a license for Casanovas, and that it is! It will destroy a woman's—*meal ticket!*"

Chaos! Now the fat was in the fire. It had perhaps been an unfortunate choice of phrase—meal ticket—but at any rate, the whole congregation, or mob, was on its feet.

Pamela's adrenaline rose to meet it. She realized also that she had to protect herself, because the atmosphere had suddenly turned nasty and hostile. But she was not alone: at least four women, all neighbors and all somewhat middle-aged like Pamela, were on her side, and Pamela saw that the armies were ranging themselves in groups, or knots. Voices rose still higher. Hymnals began to fly.

Splot!

"*Reactionaries!*"

". . . home-breakers!"

"I suppose you're anti-abortion, too!"

An egg hit Pamela between the eyes. She wiped her face with a paper tissue. Where had the egg come from? But of course many of the women had their shopping bags with them.

Tomatoes arced like red bombs through the air. Apples also. The din resembled a loud cackling of hens or of some other kind of bird, much disturbed, within a confined space. The sides were not lined up. Groups fought among one another at close range.

Whop! That had been a tin of something walloped over a woman's head in retaliation for—so the attacker averred—a worse offense. Umbrellas, at least three or four, were being brought into play now.

"Listen to what I'm *saying!*"

"You *bitch!*"

"Stop the *fighting!*"

"Everybody sit down! Where's the chairwoman?"

Some women were leaving, Pamela saw, making a crush at the front doors. Then to her own surprise, she found she had a sturdy faldstool in her hands and was about to hurl it. How many had she thrown already? Pamela dropped the stool (on her own toes) and ducked just in time to avoid being hit by a cabbage.

But it was a two-pound tin of baked beans that did for Pamela, catching her smack in her right temple. She died within a few seconds, and her assailant was never identified.

The Fully Licensed Whore, or,
the Wife

Sarah had always played the field as an amateur, and at twenty she got married, which made her licensed. To top it, the marriage was in a church in full view of family, friends and neighbors, maybe even God as witness, for certainly He was invited. She was all in white, though hardly a virgin, being two months pregnant and not by the man she was marrying, whose name was Sylvester. Now she could become a professional, with protection of the law, approval of society, blessing of the clergy, and financial support guaranteed by her husband.

Sarah lost no time. It was first the gas meter reader, to limber herself up, then the window cleaner, whose job took a varying number of hours, depending on how dirty she told Sylvester the windows had been. Sylvester sometimes had to pay for eight hours' work plus a bit of overtime. Sometimes the window cleaner was there when Sylvester left for work, and still there when he came home in the evening. But these were small fry, and Sarah progressed to their lawyer, which had the advantage of "no fee" for any services performed for the Sylvester Dillon family, now three.

Sylvester was proud of baby son Edmund, and flushed with pleasure at what friends said about Edmund's resemblance to himself. The friends were not lying, only saying what they thought they should say, and what they would have said to any father. After Edmund's birth, Sarah ceased sexual relations with Sylvester (not that they'd ever had much) saying, "One's enough, don't you think?" She could also say, "I'm tired," or "It's too hot." In plain fact, poor Sylvester was good only for his money—he wasn't wealthy but quite comfortably off—and because he was reasonably intelligent and presentable, not aggressive enough to be a nuisance and—Well, that was about all it took to satisfy Sarah. She had a vague idea that she needed a protector and escort. It somehow carried more weight to write "Mrs." at the foot of letters.

She enjoyed three or four years of twiddling about with the lawyer, then their doctor, then a couple of maverick husbands in their social circle, plus a few two-week sprees with the father of

Edmund. These men visited the house mainly during the afternoons Monday to Friday. Sarah was most cautious and insisted—her house front being visible to several neighbors—that her lovers ring her when they were already in the vicinity, so she could tell them if the coast was clear enough for them to nip in. One-thirty P.M. was the safest time, when most people were eating lunch. After all, Sarah's bed and board was at stake, and Sylvester was becoming restless, though as yet not at all suspicious.

Sylvester in the fourth year of marriage made a slight fuss. His own advances to his secretary and also to the girl who worked behind the counter in his office supplies shop had been gently but firmly rejected, and his ego was at a low ebb.

"Can't we try again?" was Sylvester's theme.

Sarah counterattacked like a dozen battalions whose guns had been primed for years to fire. One would have thought she was the one to whom injustice had been done. "Haven't I created a lovely home for you? Aren't I a good hostess—the *best* according to all our friends, isn't that true? Have I ever neglected Edmund? Have I ever failed to have a hot meal waiting for you when you come home?"

I wish you would forget the hot meal now and then and think of something else, Sylvester wanted to say, but was too well brought up to get the words out.

"Furthermore I have taste," Sarah added as a final volley. "Our furniture is not only good, it's well cared for. I don't know what more you can expect from me."

The furniture was so well polished, the house looked like a museum. Sylvester was often shy about dirtying ashtrays. He would have liked more disorder and a little more warmth. How could he say this?

"Now come and eat something," Sarah said more sweetly, extending a hand in a burst of contact unprecedented for Sylvester in the past many years. A thought had just crossed her mind, a plan.

Sylvester took her hand gladly, and smiled. He ate second helpings of everything that she pressed upon him. The dinner was as usual good, because Sarah was an excellent and meticulous cook. Sylvester was hoping for a happy end to the evening also, but in this he was disappointed.

Sarah's idea was to kill Sylvester with good food, with kindness in a sense, with wifely *duty*. She was going to cook more and more elaborately. Sylvester already had a paunch, the doctor had cautioned him about overeating, not enough exercise and all that rot, but Sarah knew enough about weight control to know that it was what you ate that counted, not how much exercise you took. And Sylvester loved to eat. The stage was set, she felt, and what had she to lose?

She began to use richer fats, goose fat, olive oil, and to make macaroni and cheese, to butter sandwiches more thickly, to push milk-drinking as a splendid source of calcium for Sylvester's falling hair. He put on twenty pounds in three months. His tailor had to alter all his suits, then make new suits for him.

"Tennis, darling," Sarah said with concern. "What you need is a bit of exercise." She was hoping he'd have a heart attack. He now weighed nearly 225 pounds, and he was not a tall man. He was already breathing hard at the slightest exertion.

Tennis didn't do it. Sylvester was wise enough, or heavy enough, just to stand there on the court and let the ball come to him, and if the ball didn't come to him, he wasn't going to run after it to hit it. So one warm Saturday, when Sarah had accompanied him to the courts as usual, she pretended to faint. She mumbled that she wanted to be taken to the car to go home. Sylvester struggled, panting, as Sarah was no lightweight herself. Unfortunately for Sarah's plans, two chaps came running from the club bar to give assistance, and Sarah was loaded easily into the Jag.

Once at home, with the front door closed, Sarah swooned again, and mumbled in a frantic but waning voice that she had to be taken upstairs to bed. It was their bed, a big double one, and two flights up. Sylvester heaved her into his arms, thinking that he did not present a romantic picture trudging up step by step, gasping and stumbling as he carried his beloved towards bed. At last he had to maneuver her onto one shoulder, and even then he fell on his own face upon reaching the landing on the second floor. Wheezing mightily, he rolled out from under her limp figure, and tried again, this time simply dragging her along the carpeted hall and into the bedroom. He was tempted to let her lie there until he got his own breath back (she wasn't stirring), but he could anticipate her recrimination if she woke up in the next seconds and found he had left her flat on the floor.

Sylvester bent to the task again, put all his will power into it, for certainly he had no physical strength left. His legs ached, his back was killing him, and it amazed him that he could get this burden (over 150 pounds) onto the double bed. "Whoosh-sh!" Sylvester said, and went reeling back, intending to collapse in an armchair, but the armchair had rollers and retreated several inches, causing him to land on the floor with a house-shaking thump. A terrible pain had struck his chest. He pressed a fist against his breast and bared his teeth in agony.

Sarah watched. She lay on the bed. She did nothing. She waited and waited. She almost fell asleep. Sylvester was moaning, calling for help. How lucky, Sarah thought, that Edmund was parked out with a baby-sitter this afternoon, instead of a baby-sitter being in the house. After some fifteen minutes, Sylvester was still. Sarah did fall asleep finally. When she got up, she found that Sylvester was quite dead and becoming cool. Then she telephoned the family doctor.

All went well for Sarah. People said that just weeks before, they'd been amazed at how *well* Sylvester looked, rosy cheeks and all that. Sarah got a tidy sum from the insurance company, her widow's pension, and gushes of sympathy from people who assured her she had given Sylvester the best of herself, had made a lovely home for him, had given him a son, had in short devoted herself utterly to him and made his somewhat short life as happy as a man's life could possibly have been. No one said, "What a perfect murder!" which was Sarah's private opinion, and now she could chuckle over it. Now she could become the Merry Widow. By exacting small favors from her lovers—casually of course—it was going to be easy to live in even better style than when Sylvester had been alive. And she could still write "Mrs." at the foot of letters.

The Breeder

To Elaine, marriage meant children. Marriage meant a lot of other things too, of course, such as creating a home, being a morale-booster to her husband, jolly companion, all that. But most of all children—that was what marriage was for, what it was all about.

Elaine, when she married Douglas, set about becoming the creature of her imagination, and within four months she had succeeded quite well. Their home sparkled with cleanliness and charm, their parties were successes, and Douglas received a small promotion in his firm, Athens Insurance Inc. Only one thing was missing, Elaine was not yet pregnant. A consultation with her doctor soon set this problem to rights, something having been askew, but after another three months, she still had not conceived. Could it be Douglas's fault? Reluctantly, somewhat shyly, Douglas visited the doctor and was pronounced fit. What could be wrong? Closer tests were made, and it was discovered that the fertilized egg (indeed at least one egg had been fertilized) had traveled upward instead of downward, in apparent defiance of gravity, and instead of developing somewhere had simply vanished.

"She should get out of bed and stand on her head!" said a wag of Douglas's office, after a couple of drinks one lunchtime.

Douglas chuckled politely. But maybe there was something to it. Hadn't the doctor said something along these lines? Douglas suggested the headstand to Elaine that evening.

Around midnight, Elaine jumped out of bed and stood on her head, feet against the wall. Her face became bright pink. Douglas was alarmed, but Elaine stuck it out like a Spartan, collapsing finally after nearly ten minutes in a rosy heap on the floor.

Their first child, Edward, was thus born. Edward started the ball rolling, and slightly less than a year later came twins, two girls. The parents of Elaine and Douglas were delighted. To become grandparents was as great a joy for them as it had been to become parents, and both sets of grandparents threw parties. Douglas and Elaine were only children, so the grandparents rejoiced that their lines would be continued. Elaine no longer had to stand on her head. And ten months later, a second son was born, Peter. Then came Philip, then Madeleine.

This made six small children in the household, and Elaine and Douglas had to move to a slightly larger apartment with one more room in it. They moved hastily, not realizing that their landlord was rather against children (they'd lied and told him they had four), especially little ones who howled in the night. Within six months, they were asked to leave—it being obvious then that Elaine was due to have another child soon. By now, Douglas was feeling the pinch, but his parents gave him $2,000 and Elaine's parents came up with $3,000, and Douglas made a down payment on a house fifteen minutes' drive from his office.

"I'm glad we've got a house, darling," he said to Elaine. "But I'm afraid we've got to watch our pennies if we keep up the mortgage payments. I think—at least for a while—we ought not to have any more children. Seven, after all—" Little Thomas had arrived.

Elaine had said before that it would be up to her, not him, to do the family planning. "I understand, Douglas. You're perfectly right."

Alas, Elaine disclosed one overcast winter day that she was pregnant again. "I can't account for it. I'm on the pill, you know that."

Douglas had certainly assumed that. He was speechless for a few moments. How were they going to manage? He could already see that Elaine was pregnant, though he'd been trying to convince himself for days that he was only imagining it, because of his anxiety. Already their parents were handing out fifty- and one-hundred-dollar presents on birthdays—with nine birthdays in the family, birthdays came along pretty frequently—and he knew they couldn't contribute a bit more. It was amazing how much shoes alone could cost for seven little ones.

Still, when Douglas saw the beatific, contented smile on Elaine's face as she lay against her pillows in the hospital, a baby boy in one arm and a baby girl in the other, Douglas could not find it in himself to regret these births, which made nine.

But they'd been married just a little more than seven years. If this kept up—

One woman in their social circle remarked at a party, "Oh, Elaine gets pregnant every time Doug *looks* at her!"

Douglas was not amused by the implied tribute to his virility.

"Then they ought to make love with the lights out!" replied the office wag. "Ha-ha-ha! Easy to see the only reason is, Douglas is *looking* at her!"

"Don't even glance at Elaine tonight, Doug!" someone else yelled, and there were gales of laughter.

Elaine smiled prettily. She imagined, nay, she was sure, that women envied her. Women with only one child, or no children, were just dried-up beanbags in Elaine's opinion. Green beanbags.

Things went from bad to worse, from Douglas's point of view. There *was* an interval of a whole six months when Elaine was on the pill and did not become pregnant, but then suddenly she was.

"I can't understand it," she said to Douglas and to her doctor too. Elaine really couldn't understand it, because she had forgotten that she had forgotten to remember the pill—a phenomenon that her doctor had encountered before.

The doctor made no comment. His lips were ethically sealed.

As if in revenge for Elaine's absenting herself from fecundity for a while, for her trying to put a lid on nature's cornucopia, nature hurled quintuplets at her. Douglas could not even face the hospital, and took to his bed for forty-eight hours. Then he had an idea: he would ring up some newspapers, ask them a fee for interviews and also for any photographs they might take of the quints. He made painful efforts in this direction, such exploitation being against his grain. But the newspapers didn't bite. Lots of people had quintuplets these days, they said. Sextuplets might interest them, but quints no. They'd take a photograph, but they wouldn't pay anything. The photograph only brought literature from family planning organizations and unpleasant or downright insulting letters from individual citizens telling Douglas and Elaine how much they were contributing to pollution. The newspapers had mentioned that their children now numbered fourteen after about eight years of marriage.

Since it seemed the pill was not working, Douglas proposed that he do something about himself. Elaine was dead against it.

"Why, things just wouldn't be the same!" she cried.

"Darling, everything would be the same. Only—"

Elaine interrupted. They got nowhere.

They had to move again. The house was big enough for two adults and fourteen children, but the added expense of the quints made the mortgage payments impossible. So Douglas and Elaine and Edward, Susan and Sarah, Peter, Thomas, Philip and Madeleine, the twins Ursula and Paul, and the quints Louise, Pamela, Helen, Samantha and Brigid moved to a tenement in the city—tenement being a legal term for any structure housing more than two families, but in common parlance a tenement was a slum, which this was. Now they were surrounded by families with nearly as many children as they had. Douglas, who sometimes took papers home from the office, stuffed his ears with cotton wool and thought he would go mad. "No danger of going mad, if I *think* I'm going mad," he told himself, and tried to cheer up. Elaine, after all, was on the pill again.

But she became pregnant again. By now, the grandparents were no longer so delighted. It was plain that the number of off-spring had lowered Douglas's and Elaine's standard of living— the last thing the grandparents wished. Douglas lived in a smoldering resentment against fate, and with a desperate hope that something—something unknown and perhaps impossible might happen, as he watched Elaine growing stouter day by day. Might this be quints again? Even sextuplets? Dreadful thought. What was the matter with the pill? Was Elaine some exception to the laws of chemistry? Douglas turned over in his mind their doctor's ambiguous reply to his question on this point. The doctor had been so vague, Douglas had forgotten not only the doctor's words, but even the sense of what he'd said. Who could think in all the noise, anyway? Diaper-clad midgets played tiny xylophones and tootled on a variety of horns and whistles. Edward and Peter squabbled over who was going to mount the rocking horse. All the girls burst into tears over nothing, hoping to gain their mother's attention and allegiance to their causes. Philip was prone to colic. All the quints were teething simultaneously.

This time it was triplets. Unbelievable! Three rooms of their flat now had nothing but cribs in them, plus a single bed in each, in which at least two children slept. If their ages only varied more, Douglas thought, it would somehow be more tolerable, but most of them were still crawling around on the floor, and to open the apartment door was to believe that one had come upon a day nursery by mistake. But no. All these seventeen were his own doing. The new triplets swung in an ingenious suspended playpen, there being absolutely no room on the floor for them. They were fed, and their nappies changed, through bars of the pen, which made Douglas think of a zoo.

Weekends were hell. Their friends simply did not accept invitations any longer. Who could blame them? Elaine had to ask guests to be very quiet, and even so, something always woke one of the little ones by 9 P.M. and then the whole lot started yowling, even the seven- and eight-year-olds who wanted to join the party. So their social life became nil, which was just as well, because they hadn't the money for entertaining.

"But I do feel fulfilled, dear," Elaine said, laying a soothing hand upon Douglas's brow, as he sat poring over office papers one Sunday afternoon.

Douglas, perspiring from nerves, was working in a tiny corner of what they called their living room. Elaine was half-dressed, her usual state, because in the act of dressing, some child always interrupted her, demanding something, and also Elaine

was still nursing the last arrivals. Suddenly something snapped in
Douglas, and he got up and walked out to the nearest telephone.
He and Elaine had no telephone, and they had had to sell their
car also.

Douglas rang a clinic and inquired about vasectomy. He was
told there was a waiting list of four months, if he wanted the operation free of charge. Douglas said yes, and gave his name.
Meanwhile, chastity was the order of the day. No hardship. Good
God! Seventeen now! Douglas hung his head in the office. Even
the jokes had worn thin. He felt that people pitied him, and that
they avoided the subject of children. Only Elaine was happy. She
seemed to be in another world. She'd even begun to talk like the
kids. Douglas counted the days till the operation. He was not
going to say anything to Elaine about it, just have it. He rang up a
week before the date to confirm it, and was told he would have to
wait another three months, because the person who had fixed his
appointment must have made a mistake.

Douglas banged the telephone down. It wasn't abstinence that
was the problem, just goddamned fate, just the nuisance of waiting
another three months. He had an insane fear that Elaine would
become pregnant again on her own.

It happened that the first thing he saw when he entered the
apartment that afternoon was little Ursula waddling around in her
rubber panties, diligently pushing a miniature pram in which sat a
tiny replica of herself.

"*Look at it!*" Douglas yelled at no one. "Motherhood already
and she can hardly *walk!*" He snatched the doll out of the toy pram
and hurled it through a window.

"Doug! What's come over you?" Elaine rushed towards him
with one breast bared, baby Charles clamped to it like a lamprey.

Douglas pushed a foot through the side of a crib, then seized
the rocking horse and smashed it against a wall. He kicked a doll's
house into the air and when it fell, demolished it with a stomp.

"*Maa-aa*—maa-aa!"

"Daa-aaddy!"

"Ooooo-ooo!"

"Boo-hooo-oo-oo-hoo-oo!" from a half dozen throats.

Now the household was in an uproar with at least fifteen kids screaming, plus Elaine. Toys were Douglas's targets. Balls of all sizes went through the windowpanes, followed by plastic horns and little pianos, cars and telephones, then teddy bears, rattles, guns, rubber swords and peashooters, teething rings and jigsaw puzzles. He squeezed two formula bottles and laughed with lunatic glee as the milk spurted from the rubber teats. Elaine's expression changed from surprise to horror. She leaned out of a broken window and screamed.

Douglas had to be dragged away from an Erector set construction which he was smashing with the heavy base of a roly-poly clown. An intern gave him a punch in the neck which knocked him out. The next thing Douglas knew, he was in a padded cell somewhere. He demanded a vasectomy. They gave him a needle instead. When he woke up, he again yelled for a vasectomy. His wish was granted the same day.

He felt better then, calmer. He was just sane enough, however, to realize that his mind, so to speak, was "gone." He was aware that he didn't want to go back to work, didn't want to do anything. He didn't want to see any of his old friends, all of whom he felt he had lost, anyway. He didn't particularly want to go on living. Dimly, he remembered that he was a laughingstock for having begotten seventeen children in not nearly so many years. Or was it nineteen? Or twenty-eight? He'd lost count.

Elaine came to see him. Was she pregnant again? No. Impossible. It was just that he was so used to seeing her pregnant. She seemed remote. She was fulfilled, Douglas remembered.

"Stand on your head again. Reverse things," Douglas said with a foolish smile.

"He's mad," Elaine said hopelessly to the intern, and calmly turned away.

The Mobile Bed-Object

There are lots of girls like Mildred, homeless, yet never without a roof—most of the time the ceiling of a hotel room, sometimes that of bachelor digs, of a yacht's cabin if they're lucky, a tent, or a caravan. Such girls are bed-objects, the kind of thing one acquires like a hot water bottle, a traveling iron, an electric shoe-shiner, any little luxury of life. It is an advantage to them if they can cook a bit, but they certainly don't have to talk, in any language. Also they are interchangeable, like unblocked currency or international postal reply coupons. Their value can go up or down, depending on their age and the man currently in possession.

Mildred considered it not a bad life, and if interviewed would have said in her earnest way, "It's *interesting.*" Mildred never laughed, and smiled only when she thought she should be polite. She was five feet seven, blondish, rather slender, with a pleasant blank face and large blue eyes which she held wide open. She slunk rather than walked, her shoulders hunched, hips thrust a bit forward—the way the best models walked, she had read somewhere. This gave her a languid, pacific air. Ambulant, she looked as if she were walking in her sleep. She was a little more lively in bed, and this fact traveled by word of mouth, or among men who might not speak the same tongue, by nods or small smiles. Mildred knew her job, and it must be said for her that she applied herself diligently to it.

She had floundered around in school till fourteen, when everyone including her parents had deemed it senseless for her to continue. She would marry early, her parents thought. Instead, Mildred ran away from home, or rather was taken away by a car salesman when she was barely fifteen. Under the salesman's direction, she wrote reassuring letters home, saying she had a job in a nearby town as a waitress and was living in a flat with two other girls.

By the time she was eighteen, Mildred had been to Capri, Mexico City, Paris, even Japan, and to Brazil several times, where men usually dumped her, since they were often on the run from something. She had been a second prize, as it were, for one American President-elect the night of his victory. She had been lent for two days to a sheik in London, who had rewarded her with a rather kinky gold goblet which she had subsequently lost—not that she liked the goblet, but it must have been worth a fortune, and she often thought of its loss with regret. If she ever wished to change her man, she would simply visit an expensive bar in Rio or anywhere, on her own, and pick up another man who would be pleased to add her to his expense account, and back she would go to America or Germany or Sweden. Mildred couldn't have cared less what country she was in.

Once she was forgotten at a restaurant table, as a cigarette lighter might be left behind. Mildred noticed, but Herb didn't for some thirty minutes which were mildly worrying for Mildred, though Mildred never got really distressed about anything. She did turn to the man sitting next to her—it was a business lunch, four men, four girls—and she said, "I thought Herb had just gone to the loo—"

"What?" The heavyset man next to her was an American. "Oh. He'll be back. We had some unpleasant business to talk over today, you know. Herb's upset." The American smiled understandingly. He had his girlfriend by his side, one he'd picked up last night. The girls hadn't opened their mouths, except to eat.

Herb came back and got Mildred, and they went to their hotel room, Herb in utmost gloom, because he'd come out badly in the business deal. Mildred's embraces that afternoon failed to lift Herb's spirits or his ego, and that evening Mildred was traded in. Her new guardian was Stanley, about thirty-five, pudgy, like Herb. The trade took place at cocktail time, while Mildred sipped her usual Alexander through a straw. Herb got Stanley's girl, a dumb blonde with artificially curled hair. The blondness was artificial too, though a good job, Mildred observed, make-up and hair-do being matters Mildred was an expert in. Mildred returned to the hotel briefly to pack her suitcase, then she spent the evening and night with Stanley. He hardly talked to her, but he smiled a lot, and made a lot of telephone calls. This was in Des Moines.

With Stanley, Mildred went to Chicago, where Stanley had a small flat of his own, plus a wife in a house somewhere, he said. Mildred wasn't worried about the wife. Only once in her life had she had to deal with a difficult wife who crashed into a flat. Mildred had brandished a carving knife, and the wife had fled. Usually a wife just looked dumbfounded, then sneered and walked off, obviously intending to avenge herself on her husband. Stanley was away all day and didn't give her much money, which was annoying. Mildred wasn't going to stay long with Stanley, if she could help it. She'd started a savings account in a bank somewhere once, but she'd lost her passbook and forgotten the name of the town where the bank was.

But before Mildred could make a wise move away from Stanley, she found herself given away. This was a shock. An economist would have drawn a conclusion about currency that was given away, and so did Mildred. She realized that Stanley came out a bit better in the deal he had made with the man called Louis, to whom he gave Mildred, but still—

And she was only twenty-three. But Mildred knew that was the danger age, and that she'd better play her cards carefully from now on. Eighteen was the peak, and she was five years past it, and what had she to show for it? A diamond bracelet that men eyed with greed, and that she'd twice had to get out of hock with the aid of some new bastard. A mink coat—same story. A suitcase with a couple of good-looking dresses. What did she want? Well, she wanted to continue the same life but with a sense of greater security. What would she do if her back was really to the wall? If she, kicked out maybe, not even given away, had to go to a bar and even then couldn't pick up more than a one-night stand? Well, she had some addresses of past men-friends, and she could always write them and threaten to put them in her memoirs, which she could say a publisher was paying her to write. But Mildred had talked with girls twenty-five and older who'd threatened memoirs, if they weren't pensioned off for life, and she'd heard of only one who had succeeded. More often, the girls said, it was a laugh they got, or a "Go ahead and write it" rather than any money.

So Mildred made the best of it for a few days with fat old Louis. He had a nice tabby cat, of which Mildred grew fond, but the most boring thing was that his apartment was a one-room kitchenette and dreary. Louis was good-natured but tightfisted. Also it was embarrassing for Mildred to be sneaked out when she and Louis went out for dinner (not usually, because Louis expected her to cook and to do a little cleaning too), and when Louis had people in to talk business, to be asked to hide in the kitchenette and not to make a sound. Louis sold pianos wholesale. Mildred rehearsed the speech she was going to make soon: "I hope you realize you haven't any hold over me, Louis . . . I'm a girl who's not used to working, not even in bed . . ."

But before she had a chance to make her speech, which would mainly have been a demand for more money, because she knew Louis had plenty tucked away, she was given away to a young salesman one night. Louis simply said, after they'd all finished dinner in a roadside café, "Dave, why don't you take Mildred to your place for a nightcap? I've got to turn in early." With a wink.

Dave beamed. He was nice-looking, but he lived in a caravan, good God! Mildred had no intention of becoming a *gypsy*, taking sponge baths, enduring portable loos. She was used to grand hotels with room service day and night. Dave might be young and ardent, but Mildred didn't give a damn about that. Men said women were all alike, but in her opinion it was even truer that men were all alike. All they wanted was one thing. Women at least wanted fur coats, good perfume, a holiday in the Bahamas, a cruise somewhere, jewelry—in fact, quite a number of things.

One evening when she was with Dave at a business dinner (he was a piano distributor and order-taker, though Mildred never saw a piano around the caravan), Mildred made the acquaintance of a

Mr. Zupp, called Sam, who had invited Dave to dine in a fancy restaurant. Inspired by three Alexanders, Mildred flirted madly with Sam, who was not unresponsive under the table, and Mildred simply announced that she was going home with Sam. Dave's mouth fell open, and he started to make a fuss, but Sam—an older, more self-assured man—most diplomatically implied that he would make a scene if it came to a fistfight, so Dave backed down.

This was a big improvement. Sam and Mildred flew at once to Paris, then to Hamburg. Mildred got new clothes. The hotel rooms were great. Mildred never knew from one day to the next what town they would be in. Now here was a man whose memoirs would be worth something, if she could only find out what he did. But when he spoke on the telephone, it was either in code, or in Yiddish, or Russian, or Arabic. Mildred had never heard such baffling languages in her life, and she was never able to find out just what he was selling. People had to sell something, didn't they? Or buy something, and if they bought something, there had to be a source of money, didn't there? So what was even the source of money? Something told Mildred that it would soon be time for her to retire. Sam Zupp seemed to have been sent by Providence. She worked on him, trying to be subtle.

"I wouldn't mind settling down," she said.

"I'm not the marrying kind," he retorted with a smile.

That wasn't what she meant. She meant a nest egg, and then he could say good-bye, if he wanted to. But wouldn't it take a few nest eggs to make a big nest egg? Would she have to go through all this again with future Sam Zupps? Mildred's mind staggered with the effort to see so far into the future, but there seemed no doubt that she should take advantage of Mr. Zupp, at least, while she had him. These ideas, or plans, frail as damaged spider webs, were swept away by the events of the days after the above conversation.

Sam Zupp was suddenly on the run. For a few days, it was airplanes with separate seats, because he and Mildred were not supposed to be traveling together. Once police sirens were behind them, as Sam's hired driver zoomed and careered over an Alpine road, bound for Geneva. Or maybe Zurich. Mildred was in her element, ministering to Sam with handkerchiefs moistened in eau de cologne, producing a *sandwich de jambon* out of her handbag in case he was hungry, or a flask of brandy if he felt his heart fluttering. Mildred fancied herself one of the heroines she had seen in films— good films—about men and their girlfriends fleeing from the awful and so unfairly well-armed police.

Her daydreams of glamour were brief. It must have been in Holland—Mildred didn't know where she was half the time— when the chauffeur-driven car suddenly screeched to a halt, just like in the films, and Mildred was bundled by both chauffeur and Sam into a mummy-like casing of stiff, heavy tarpaulin, and then ropes were tied around her. She was dumped into a canal and drowned.

No one ever heard of Mildred. No one ever found her. If she had been found, there would have been no immediate means of identification, because Sam had her passport, and her handbag was in the car. She had been thrown away, as one might throw away a Cricket Lighter when it is used up, like a paperback one has read and which has become excess baggage. Mildred's absence was never taken seriously by anyone. The score or so people who knew and remembered her, themselves scattered about the world, simply thought she was living in some other country or city. One day, they supposed, she'd turn up again in some bar, in some hotel lobby. Soon they forgot her.

The Perfect Little Lady

Theadora, or Thea as she was called, was the perfect little lady born. Everyone said that who had seen her from her first months of life, when she was being wheeled about in her white satin-lined pram. She slept when she should have slept. Then she woke and smiled at strangers. She almost never wet her diapers. She was the easiest child in the world to toilet train, and she learned to speak remarkably early. Next came reading when she was hardly two. And always she showed good manners. At three, she began to curtsy on being introduced to people. Her mother taught her this, of course, but Thea took to etiquette like a duck to water.

"Thank you, I had a lovely time," she was saying glibly at four, dropping a farewell curtsy, on departing from children's parties. She would return home with her little starched dress as neat and clean as when she had put it on. She took great care of her hair and nails. She was never dirty, and she watched other children running and playing, making mud pies, falling and skinning their knees, and she thought them utterly silly. Thea was an only child. Other mothers, more harassed than Thea's mother, with two or three offspring to look after, praised Thea's obedience and neatness, and Thea loved this. Thea basked also in the praise she got from her own mother. Thea and her mother adored each other.

Among Thea's contemporaries, the gang age began at eight or nine or ten, if the word gang could be used for the informal group that roved the neighborhood on roller skates and bicycles. It was a proper middle-class neighborhood. But if a child didn't join in the "crazy poker" game in the garage of one of their parents, or go on aimless follow-my-leader bicycle rides through the residential streets, that child was nowhere. Thea was nowhere, as far as this gang went. "I couldn't care less, because I don't want to be one of *them,* anyway," Thea said to her mother and father.

"Thea cheats at games. That's why we don't want her," said a ten-year-old boy in one of Thea's father's history classes.

Thea's father Ted taught in a local grade school. He had long suspected the truth, but had kept his mouth shut and hoped for the best. Thea was a mystery to Ted. How could he, such an ordinary, plodding fellow, have begotten a full-blown woman?

"Little girls are born women," said Thea's mother Margot. "But little boys are not born men. They have to learn to be men. Little girls have already a woman's character."

"But this isn't character," Ted said. "It's scheming. Character takes time to be formed. Like a tree."

Margot smiled tolerantly, and Ted had the feeling he was talking like someone from the Stone Age, while his wife and daughter lived in the jet age.

Thea's main objective in life seemed to be to make her contemporaries feel awful. She'd told a lie about another little girl, in regard to a little boy, and the little girl had wept and nearly had a nervous breakdown. Ted couldn't remember the details, though he'd been able to follow the story when he had heard it first, summarized by Margot. Thea had managed to blame the other little girl for the whole thing. Machiavelli couldn't have done better.

"She's simply not a ruffian," said Margot. "Anyway, she's got Craig to play with, so she's not alone."

Craig was ten and lived three houses away. What Ted did not realize for a while was that Craig was ostracized too, and for the same reason. One afternoon, Ted observed one of the boys of the neighborhood make a rude gesture, in ominous silence, as he passed Craig on the pavement.

"Scum!" Craig replied promptly. Then he trotted, in case the other boy gave chase, but the other boy simply turned and said:

"And you're a *shit,* like Thea!"

It was not the first time that Ted had heard such language from the local kids, but he certainly didn't hear it often, and he was impressed.

"But what do they do—all alone, Thea and Craig?" Ted asked his wife.

"Oh, they take walks. I dunno," said Margot. "I suppose Craig has a slight crush on her."

Ted had thought of that. Thea had a candy-box prettiness that would assure her of boyfriends by the time she reached her early teens, and of course Thea was starting earlier than that. Ted had no fear of misbehavior on Thea's part, because she was the teasing type, and basically prim.

What Thea and Craig were then engaged in was observing the construction of a dugout, tunnel and two fireplaces in a vacant lot about a mile away. Thea and Craig would go there on their bicycles, conceal themselves in the bushes nearby, and spy and giggle. A dozen or so of the gang were working like navvies, hauling out buckets of earth, gathering firewood, preparing roasted potatoes with salt and butter, which was the high point of all this slavery, around 6 P.M. Thea and Craig intended to wait until the excavation and embellishments were completed, and then they meant to smash the whole thing.

Meanwhile, Thea and Craig came up with what they called "a new ballgame," this being their code word for a nasty scheme. They sent a typewritten announcement to the biggest blabbermouth of the school, Veronica, saying that a girl called Jennifer was having a surprise birthday party on a certain date, and please tell everyone, but don't tell Jennifer. The letter was presumably from Jennifer's mother. Then Thea and Craig hid in the hedges and watched their schoolmates turn up at Jennifer's, some dressed in their best, nearly all bearing gifts, as Jennifer grew more and more embarrassed on the doorstep, saying she didn't know anything about a party. Since Jennifer's family was well-to-do, all the kids had expected a big evening.

When the tunnel and dugout, fireplaces and candle niches were all completed, Thea and Craig in their respective homes pretended bellyaches one day, and did not go to school. By prearrangement, they sneaked out and met at 11 A.M. with their bicycles. They went to the dugout and jumped in unison on the tunnel top until it caved in. Then they broke the chimney tops, and scattered the carefully gathered firewood. They even found the potatoes and salt reserve, and flung that into the woods. Then they cycled home.

Two days later, on Thursday which was a school day, Craig was found at 5 P.M. behind some elm trees on the lawn of the Knobel house, stabbed to death through the throat and heart. He had ugly wounds also about the head, as if he had been hit repeatedly by rough stones. Measurements of the knife wounds showed that at least seven different knives had been used.

Ted was profoundly shocked. By then he had heard of the destroyed tunnel and fireplaces. Everyone knew that Thea and Craig had been absent from school on the Tuesday that the tunnel had been ruined. Everyone knew that Thea and Craig were constantly together. Ted feared for his daughter's life. The police could not lay the blame for Craig's death on any member of the gang, neither could they charge an entire group with murder or manslaughter. The inquiry was concluded with a warning to all parents of the children in the school.

"Just because Craig and I were absent from school on the same day doesn't mean that we went together to break up a stupid old tunnel," said Thea to a friend of her mother's, a mother of one of the gang members. Thea could lie like an accomplished crook. It was difficult for an adult to challenge her.

So Thea's gang age, such as it was, ended with Craig's death. Then came boyfriends and teasing, opportunities for intrigues and betrayals, and a constant stream, ever changing, of young men aged sixteen to twenty, some of whom lasted only five days with Thea.

We take leave of Thea as she sits primping, aged fifteen, in front of her looking-glass. She is especially happy this evening, because her nearest rival, a girl named Elizabeth, has just been in a car accident and had her nose and jaw broken, plus an eye damaged, so she will never look quite the same again. The summer is coming up, with all those dinner dances on terraces and swimming pool parties. There is even a rumor that Elizabeth may have to acquire a lower denture, so many of her teeth got broken, but the eye damage must be the most telling. Thea, however, will escape every catastrophe. There is a divinity that protects perfect little ladies like Thea.

The Silent Mother-in-Law

This mother-in-law, Edna, has heard all the jokes about mothers-in-law, and she has no intention of being the butt of such jests, or falling into any of the traps with which her path is so amply sprinkled. First of all, she lives with her daughter and son-in-law, so she's got to be doubly or triply careful. She would never dream of criticizing anything. The young people could come home dead drunk, and Edna would never comment. They could smoke pot (in fact they do sometimes), they could fight and throw crockery at each other, and Edna wouldn't open her mouth. She's heard enough about mothers-in-law intruding, and she keeps a buttoned lip. In fact, the oddest thing about Edna is her silence. She does say, "Yes, thank you" to a second cup of coffee, and "Good night, sleep well," but that's about it.

The second outstanding thing about Edna is her thriftiness. Little does she suspect that it gives Laura and Brian a pain in the neck, because they are also trying to make the best of it, trying to be polite, and would never dream of saying that her thriftiness gives them a pain in the neck. For one thing, thrift obviously gives Edna so much pleasure. She exhibits a huge ball of saved string as other mothers-in-law might show a quilt they had made. She puts every last orange pip into a plastic bag destined for the compost heap. It would cost Laura and Brian about three hundred dollars a month to set Edna up in a flat by herself. Edna has some money which she contributes to their household, but if she lived alone, Laura and Brian would have to contribute more than she costs them now, so they let well enough alone.

Edna is fifty-six, rather lean and wiry, with short curly hair of mixed gray and black. Due to her habit of scurrying about doing things, she has a humped posture and gait. She is never idle, and seldom sits. When she does sit, it is usually because someone has asked her to, then she flings herself into a chair, and folds her hands with an attentive expression. She nearly always has something useful stewing on the stove, like apple sauce. Or she has started to clean the oven with some chemical product, which means Laura can't use the oven for at least the next hour.

Laura and Brian have no children as yet, because they are foresighted people, and in the back of their minds they are trying to think how to install Edna somewhere graciously and comfortably, even at their own expense, and after that they'll think of raising a family. All this causes a strain. Their house is a two-story affair in a suburb, twenty-five minutes' drive from the city where Brian works as an electronic engineer. He has good hopes for advancement, and is studying in his spare time at home. Edna takes a swat at the garden and lawn mowing, so Brian hasn't too much to do on weekends. But he has a feeling Edna is listening through the walls. Edna's room is next to their bedroom. There is an attic, which is unheated. In the attic, which Brian and Laura would gladly make habitable, Edna is collecting jam jars, cartons, wooden crates, old Christmas boxes and wrapping paper, and other things which might come in handy one day. Brian can't get a foot in the door now without knocking something down. He wants to have a look at the attic to see how difficult it might be to insulate and all that. The attic has become Edna's property, somehow.

"If she'd only *say* something—even now and then," Brian said one day to Laura. "It's like living with a robot."

Laura knew. She had assumed a chatty, extra pleasant manner with her mother in hopes of drawing her out. "I'll just put this here—mm-m—and the ashtray can just as well go here," Laura would say as she pottered about the house.

Edna would nod and smile a tense approval, and say nothing, though she would be hovering to help.

The atmosphere was driving Brian round the bend. He frequently muttered curses. One night when he and Laura were at a party in the neighborhood, an idea struck Brian. He told Laura his plan, and she agreed. She'd had a few drinks, and Brian told her to have another.

Laura and Brian drove home after the party, undressed in their car, walked up to the front door and pushed the bell. A long wait. They giggled. It was after 2 A.M., and Edna was in bed. Edna at last arrived and opened the door.

"Howdy doody, Edna!" said Brian, waltzing in.

"Evening, mama," said Laura.

Flustered and horrified, Edna blinked, but soon recovered enough to laugh and smile politely.

"Well, aren't you surprised? *Say* something!" Brian cried, but not being as drunk then as Laura, he seized a sofa pillow and held it so as to cover his nakedness, hating himself as he did so, for it was rather as if he had lost his guts.

Laura was executing a solo ballet, quite uninhibited.

Edna had vanished into the kitchen. Brian pursued her and saw that she was making instant coffee.

"Listen, Edna!" he shouted. "You might at least *talk* to us, no? It's simple, isn't it? Please, for the love of God, say something to us!" He was still clutching the pillow against himself, but he gesticulated with a fist of his other hand.

"It's true, mama!" Laura said from the doorway. Her eyes were full of tears. She was hysterical with conviction. "*Speak* to us!"

"I think it is disgraceful, if you want me to say something," said Edna, the longest sentence she had uttered in years. "Drunk and naked besides! I am ashamed of you both! Laura, take a raincoat from the downstairs hall, take anything! And *you*—my *son-in-law*!" Edna was shrieking.

The kettle water seethed. Edna fled past Brian and scurried upstairs to her room.

Neither Brian nor Laura remembered much of the hours after that. If they hoped they had broken Edna's silence permanently, they soon found they were wrong. Edna was just as silent as ever the next morning, Sunday, though she did smile a little—almost as if nothing had happened.

Brian went to work on Monday as usual, and when he came

home, Laura told him that Edna had been unusually busy all day. She had also been silent.

"I think she's ashamed of herself," Laura said. "She wouldn't even have lunch with me."

Brian gathered that Edna had been busy stacking firewood, cleaning the barbecue pit, peeling green apples, sewing, polishing brass, searching through a large garbage bin—for God knew what.

"What is she doing now?" Brian asked with a prickle of alarm.

At the same moment, he knew. Edna was in the attic. There was an occasional creak of floor wood from way upstairs, a *clunk* as she set down a carton of glass jars or some such.

"We should leave her alone for a bit," said Brian, feeling he was being manly and sensible.

Laura agreed.

They didn't see Edna at dinner. They went to bed. Edna seemed to work through the night, judging from the noises on the stairs and in the attic. Around dawn, a terrible crash occurred, against which Brian had once warned Laura: the attic floor was made of laths, after all, just nailed to rafters. Edna fell through the floor along with jam jars, crates, raspberry preserves, rocking chairs, an old sofa, a trunk and a sewing machine. Crash, bang, tinkle!

Brian and Laura, who had been cringing in their bed, sprang up at once to rescue Edna from the debacle, but they knew before they touched her that all was up. Poor Edna was dead. Perhaps she had not died from the fall, even, but she was dead. Thus was the rather noisy end of Brian's silent mother-in-law.

The Prude

Sharon would never, and had never, thought of herself as a prude. She considered herself simply respectable. Her mother had always said, "Be pure in every way," and when Sharon reached adolescence, her mother had emphasized the importance of being a virgin until marriage. "What else has a woman to offer a man?" was her mother's rhetorical dictum. So Sharon practiced this, and as it happened, or maybe by inevitable destiny, her husband Matthew was a virgin until marriage also. Matthew had been a hardworking law student when Sharon met him.

Now Matthew was a hardworking lawyer, and he and Sharon had three daughters, Gwen, Penny and Sybille, ranging in age from twenty down to sixteen. Sharon had always said to her women-friends, "I'll get them to the altar as virgins, if it's the last thing I do." Some of the women-friends thought Sharon was old-fashioned, others thought her hopes vain in the times in which they lived. But no one had the courage to say to Sharon that she was misplacing her energies, or even that she might be doomed to disappointment. After all, Sharon's and Matthew's attitudes were their own business, and their daughters were indeed models of young womanhood. They were polite, attractive, and doing well in their studies.

"You know, virgins are a bore," said Gwen's boyfriend to Sharon, though in a respectful tone. Toby was a bright, industrious young man, studying to become a doctor. He was twenty-three, and attended the same university as Gwen, fifty miles away. Toby had brought along two cuttings from *women*'s magazines, which he thought would impress Gwen's mother (whom he rightly supposed was the origin of Gwen's scruples). He also had a news-paper cutting on the same subject written by a man-sociologist. The authors of these statements held responsible positions in business and the professions, they weren't just beatniks, Toby pointed out. "You see, there's no reason for a girl to be unpleasantly shocked when she's married. She ought to learn something, and so should the young man. Otherwise if both are virgins, it can be an awkward and even embarrassing experience for both."

Sharon was shocked into a long silence of more than a minute. Her first impulse was to ask Toby to leave the house. She laid the cuttings to one side, on a wine table, as if the very paper they were printed on were filthy. It was plain to Sharon that all Toby wanted was *that,* whereas until now he had spoken of marriage to Gwen. He'd even spoken to Matthew, and though the engagement had not been announced in the newspapers, Sharon and her husband considered it official. The marriage was to take place next June, after Gwen's graduation. Sharon managed a small smile. "I daresay after you've—taken advantage of my daughter, you won't be interested in marrying her, will you?"

Toby leaned forward and wanted to get to his feet, but didn't. "I'm sure you think that, but it's far from the truth. If anyone won't want to get married, it might be Gwen—but that's her perfect right, to know what she's marrying. It could be that she won't like me. It's best to find out first, isn't it?"

No, Sharon thought. Marry and be stuck with it, make the best of it, was her credo. It was a *lowering of standards* . . . The right words failed her, though she was sure she was right. "I think Gwen is perhaps not the right girl for you," Sharon said finally.·

Toby's face fell. He nodded, with a stunned look. "Very well. I won't argue. I'm sorry I argued." He took back his cuttings carefully.

Gwen had stayed discreetly in the garden during this interview. At dinner, she sulked. It was summer holidays, and all three daughters were at home. The Matter was not mentioned. Toby did not come again to the house during the two weeks that remained of the holidays, but Sharon assumed that Gwen was seeing him. When Christmas holidays came, and Gwen arrived home from university, she announced to her mother that she had lost her virginity to Toby. Gwen looked radiant, though she held back her happiness as best she could, not wanting to be rudely rebellious.

Sharon turned pale and almost fainted.

"But we *are* going to be married, in just six months, Mother," Gwen said. "Now it's surer than ever. We know we like each other." Sharon told Matthew. Matthew turned grim, not knowing what to say to Gwen, therefore keeping silent.

The more serious event was that Gwen told her sisters, who had quizzed her about their parents' change of mood until Gwen did tell them. After all, thought Gwen, one sister was eighteen and the other sixteen—both old enough to be married, if they'd wished to be. Gwen's two younger sisters were enthralled, but Gwen refused to answer their questions. For Penny and Sybille, this lent an even greater mystique to Gwen's experience.

They also decided to do the same thing, because goodness knew their respective boyfriends had been besieging them with the same request. The awful blows fell upon Matthew and Sharon that season of Christmas. Penny, then the baby Sybille, came home at 2 A.M. instead of the curfew hour of midnight on two successive weekends. Penny held out against the questions of her parents, but Sybille fairly blurted to her mother that she had said "Yes," as she put it, to Frank, aged eighteen.

"You *two*," said Sharon to her daughters Penny and Sybille, "will not bring either Peter or Frank to this house again! Do you hear me?"

Then Sharon collapsed. This was the evening of the day Sybille had broken her news. The doctor was summoned. Sharon had to be given a sedative. Matthew, who in the doctor's presence had almost struck Sybille in his anger, was persuaded by the family doctor to have a sedative injection also. But unlike Sharon, Matthew was not knocked out.

"You girls will not leave the house until you have my permission to do so!" Matthew fulminated, before he staggered up the stairs to his bedroom, which was separate from his wife's.

"They have all, all given away the only thing that they have to offer a husband," said Sharon to Matthew, and she called her blonde daughters into her bedroom to say the same thing to them.

The daughters hung their heads and appeared chastened, but inwardly they were not, and outside their mother's bedroom, the middle sister Penny said to her older sister, in the presence of the young Sybille, "Isn't the whole world on our side?"

All three daughters were happy with first love.

"Yes," said Gwen, with conviction.

Meanwhile Sharon, still abed, murmured to Matthew who visited her, "All our efforts wasted. The Grand Tour of Europe—" They'd taken their daughters two years ago to Florence, Paris, Venice. "The private French lessons, the piano lessons—*civilization*—"

The doctor had to come again with sedatives, though he advised Sharon to try to walk around a bit.

Then the real blow fell. Sybille found the courage to ask her father if her boyfriend Frank could move into the house. Frank's parents were in agreement, if Matthew was. Matthew could not believe his ears. And meanwhile Frank would continue to go to junior college in town, Sybille said.

"What on earth would the neighbors *think*?" said her father. "Hasn't that ever crossed your mind?"

"Estelle's got *her* boyfriend living in the house!" replied Sybille, before fleeing her father's study. She meant the Thompsons down the street. But what was the use with such fuddy-duddies? It was enough to make anybody leave home. Her father had probably never heard of The Pill.

"I feel like throwing a bucket of water on them," said Sharon from her bed, meaning the boyfriends of all her daughters. She was remembering the times she had thrown buckets of water at besieging tomcats, but it had not protected their female Siamese cat whose bastard son was even now a member of the household.

Matthew was trying his best to hold the home together. "There is one good thing," he said. "None of our daughters is pregnant. And Gwen's wedding is going to take place." He was mindful of Estelle Thompson's family down the road, with the boyfriend living in the household. Matthew couldn't tell his wife this, it would kill her. It had made a serious breach in his own wall. But wouldn't it be better to yield a little than to be completely vanquished?

"It is not the same," replied Sharon, dismally turning her face away. "Gwen is no longer pure."

Realizing that moving Frank into the house would deeply wound her parents, Sybille moved in with Frank. This shattered Matthew, his hands trembled, and he did not go to his office for a couple of days. He was ashamed even to be seen on the street. What were the neighbors thinking?

Really, the neighbors were no longer shocked by such things, and some thought it made for stability among the young.

Penny, the middle daughter, was sharing a small flat with Peter, in their college town now, and both were doing better in their studies. This was in January and February.

In January also, Sharon heard of her baby Sybille's having moved into Frank's household. The char told her. Matthew could never have told his wife such a thing. Sharon was still in bed. She had of course missed Sybille some ten days ago, and Matthew had said Sybille had taken a suitcase and was staying with Sharon's sister in town, and still going to school. But the char said with a merry laugh, out of the blue:

"I hear Sybille's moved into her boyfriend's house. Isn't she the grown-up young lady now!" The char had assumed that Sharon knew.

Sharon, doped on sedatives, thought the char was making a cruel joke. "It's no time for laughter—or funny stories, Mabel."

"But it's *true!*" said Mabel. Then she realized that Sharon hadn't known.

"Get out of my house!" Sharon cried with all the energy she had left.

"Sorry, madam," said Mabel, and went out of the room.

Sharon got with difficulty out of bed, intending to go downstairs and speak with Matthew who was again home. At the top of the stairs, Sharon lost her grip on the banister and fell the whole length—thirty-five dreadful steps, which though carpeted, bruised her horribly. Matthew found her at the bottom a few seconds later, and at once summoned the doctor.

"She is illustrating the fall of her house," said the doctor, who was a bit of a psychiatrist and thought himself wise.

"But how badly is she injured?" Matthew asked.

Nothing was broken, but now Sharon had to stay in bed. She became weaker and weaker. So did Matthew, as if by contagion. He stopped working. Fortunately, he could afford it. He and Sharon aged rapidly in the next months. Their daughters flourished. Gwen produced a baby boy a few months after her marriage. Sybille won a scholarship because of her good work in chemistry. Penny, unmarried, still lived with Peter, and both were doing well too. They were reading sociology and studying Eastern languages with a view to doing fieldwork. They all sensed a purpose in life.

For Sharon, life had lost its purpose, because her main purpose had failed. To her, her daughters were tramps, whores in masquerade, and still, Penny and Sybille (but not Gwen), taking money from home. Matthew was caught in the crossfire. He could see that his daughters were doing well, yet he was like his wife: he did not approve. After all, he had kept his chastity until marriage. Why couldn't everyone else, especially his own daughters? He went to see an analyst, whose words seemed to split Matthew further, instead of putting him back together again. Then there was his daughter Gwen implying in her letters that *his* attitude was a trifle vulgar. Matthew wanted to commit suicide, but didn't, because he had always considered suicide a coward's act. He died in his sleep aged seventy.

Sharon lingered on to an incredible old age, ninety-nine. She had long ago forbidden her daughters the house. She now had four great-grandchildren, and had never seen either grandchildren or great-grandchildren. In senility, Sharon reverted to the past, and her dying words were, "I'll get them to the altar as virgins . . . to the altar . . ." She had to be tied in bed. It was better than falling down the stairs again.

The Victim

It started when plump, blonde little Catherine was four or five years old: her parents noticed that she got hurt, fell, or did something disastrous far more often than did her contemporaries. Why was Cathy's nose so often bleeding, her knees scraped? Why did she so often wail for mama's sympathy? Why had she broken her arm twice before she was eight? Why, indeed? Especially since Cathy was not the outdoor type. She much preferred to play indoors. For instance, she liked dressing up in her mother's clothes, when her mother was out of the house. Cathy put on long dresses, high heels, and make-up which she applied at her mother's dressing table. Two such efforts had, both times, caused Cathy to catch her wobbly shoes in her skirts and fall down the stairs. She had been en route to see herself in the long looking-glass in the living room. This had been the cause of one of the arm breaks.

Now Cathy was eleven, and had long ago stopped trying on her mother's clothes. She had her own platform boots which made her five inches taller, her own dressing table with lipsticks, pancake make-up, hair curlers, curling irons, hair rinses, artificial eyelashes, even a wig on a pedestal. The wig had cost Cathy three months' allowance, and even so her parents had chipped in twenty dollars to buy it.

"I don't know why she wants to look like a grown-up woman aged thirty," said Vic, Cathy's father. "She's got plenty of time for that."

"Oh, it's normal at her age," said her mother, Ruby, though Ruby knew it wasn't quite normal.

Cathy complained about boys pestering her. "They just won't let me alone!" she said to her parents one evening, not for the first time. "Look at these bruises!" Cathy pushed up a colorful nylon blouse to show a couple of bruises on her ribs. She tottered a little in her white platform boots, topped incongruously by yellow knee-length stockings, which would have been more appropriate for a scoutmaster.

"Kee-rist!" said Vic, who was then drying dishes. "Look at these, Ruby! You didn't just fall down somewhere, did you, Cathy?"

At the sink, Ruby was not much impressed by the blue-brown bruises. She had seen compound fractures.

"The boys just grab me and squeeze me!" Cathy whined.

Vic almost threw the plate he was drying, but finally put it gently on top of a stack in the cupboard. "What do you expect, Cathy, if you wear phony long eyelashes to school at nine in the morning? You know, Ruby, it's her own fault."

But Vic couldn't make Ruby agree. Ruby kept saying it was normal at her age, or some such. Cathy would have turned him off, Vic thought, if he'd been a boy of thirteen or fourteen. But he had to admit that Cathy looked like fair game, a pushover to any stupid adolescent boy. He tried to explain this to Ruby, and get her to exert some control.

Ruby said, "You know, Vic darling, you're being the overprotective father. It's quite a common syndrome, and I don't want to reproach you. But you must relax about Cathy or you'll make things worse."

Cathy had round blue eyes, and long lashes by nature. Her Cupid's bow mouth tended to turn up at the corners in a sweet and willing smile. In school, she was rather good at biology, at drawing spirogyra, the circulatory systems of frogs, and cross sections of carrots as seen under a microscope. Miss Reynolds, her biology teacher, liked her, lent her pamphlets and quarterlies, which Cathy read and returned.

Then in summer vacation, when Cathy was almost twelve, she began hitchhiking, for no reason. The children of the neighborhood went to a lake ten miles away, where there was swimming, fishing and canoeing.

"Cathy, don't hitchhike. It's dangerous. There's a bus twice a day, going and coming," said Vic.

But there she went, hitchhiking, like a lemming rushing to its fate, Vic thought. One of her boyfriends called Joey, aged fifteen and with a car, could have driven her, but Cathy preferred to thumb rides from truck drivers. Thus she was raped for the first time.

Cathy made a big scene at the lake, burst into tears when she arrived on foot, and said, "I've just been raped!"

Bill Owens, the caretaker, at once asked Cathy to describe the man, and the kind of truck he'd been driving.

"He was redheaded," said Cathy tearfully. "Maybe twenty-eight. He was big and strong."

Bill Owens drove Cathy in his car to the nearest hospital. Cathy was photographed by journalists, and given ice cream sodas. She told her story to journalists and the doctors.

Cathy stayed home, pampered, for three days. The mysterious redheaded rapist was never found, although the doctors confirmed that she had been raped. Then Cathy went back to school, dressed to the nines, or the hilt again—platform shoes, pancake make-up, nail polish, scent, cleavage. She acquired more bruises. The telephone in her house kept ringing: the boys wanted to ask her out. Half the time Cathy sneaked out, half the time she stood the boys up with promises, causing the boys to hang around outside the house, in cars or on foot. Vic was disgusted. But what could he do?

Ruby kept saying, "It's natural. Cathy's just popular!"

Christmas holidays came, and the family went to Mexico. They had wanted to go to Europe, but Europe was too expensive. They drove to Juarez, crossed the border, and made their way to Guadalajara on their way to Mexico City. The Mexicans, men and women alike, stared at Cathy. She was obviously still a child, yet made up like a grown woman. Vic realized why the Mexicans stared, but Ruby seemed not to.

"Creepy people, these Mexicans," said Ruby.

Vic sighed. It might have been during one of these sighs that Cathy was whisked away. Vic and Ruby had been walking along a narrow pavement, Cathy behind them, on the way to their hotel, and when they turned round, Cathy wasn't there.

"Didn't she say she was going to buy an ice cream cone?" asked Ruby, ready to run to the next street corner to see if there wasn't an ice cream vendor there.

"I didn't hear her say that," said Vic. He looked frantically in all directions. There was nothing but men in business suits, a few peasants in sombreros and white trousers—mostly carrying bundles of some kind—and respectable-looking Mexican women doing their shopping. Where was a policeman? For the next half hour, Vic and Ruby made their problem known to a couple of Mexican policemen who listened carefully and took down a description of their daughter Cathy. Vic even produced a photograph from his wallet.

"Only twelve? Really?" said one of the policemen.

Vic handed the photograph over to him and never saw it again.

Cathy returned to their hotel towards midnight. She was tired and dirty, but she made her way to the door of her parents' room. She told her parents she had been raped. Meanwhile the manager of the hotel had rung seconds before to say:

"Your daughter has returned! She went straight up in the elevator, didn't speak to us!"

Cathy said to her parents, "He was a nice-looking man, and he spoke English. He wanted me to look at a monkey he said he had in his car. *I* didn't think there was anything wrong about him."

"A *monkey*?" said Vic.

"But there wasn't any monkey," Cathy said, "and we drove off." Then she began to cry.

Vic and Ruby were dismayed at the prospect of trying to find a nice-looking man who spoke English, of trying to deal with Mexican courts if they did find him. They packed up and took Cathy back to America, hoping for the best, meaning that Cathy wasn't pregnant. She wasn't. They took Cathy to their doctor.

"It's all those cosmetics she puts on," said the doctor. "They make her look older."

Vic knew.

A real drama, however, took place the following year. Their next-door neighbors had a young doctor visiting them for a month that summer. His name was Norman, and he was a nephew of the woman of the house, Marian. Cathy told Norman she wanted to become a nurse, and Norman lent her books, and spent hours with her, talking about medicine and the nursing profession. Then one afternoon, Cathy ran into her house in tears and told her mother that Norman had been seducing her for weeks, and that he wanted her to run away with him, and had threatened to kidnap her if she didn't.

Ruby was shocked—and yet somehow *not* shocked, but more embarrassed. Ruby might have chosen to confine Cathy to the house, to say nothing about the story, but Cathy had already told Marian.

Marian arrived just two minutes after Cathy. "I don't know what to say! It's dreadful! I can't believe it of Norman, but it must be true. He's fled the house. He packed his suitcase in a flash, but he's left a few things behind."

This time, Cathy did not cease her tears, but kept them flowing for days. She told stories of Norman forcing her to do things she couldn't bring herself to describe. Word got around in the neighborhood. Norman was not in his apartment in Chicago, Marian said, because she had tried to ring him and there was no answer. A police hunt was mounted—though who initiated it, no one knew. Vic hadn't, nor Ruby, Marian nor her husband.

Norman was at last found holed up in a hotel hundreds of miles away. He had registered under his own name. A charge was made by police in the name of a government committee for the protection of minors. A trial began in Cathy's town. Cathy enjoyed every minute of it. She went to court daily, whether she had to testify or not, primly dressed, without make-up or artificial eyelashes, but she could not straighten her permanented hair, whose ultra-blondeness was starting to grow out, showing darker hair at the roots. When on the stand, she pretended she could not force the awful facts from her lips, so the prosecuting lawyer had to suggest them, and Cathy murmured "Yes," which she was often asked to say louder, so the court could hear. People shook their heads, hissed Norman, and by the end of the trial were in a mood to lynch him. All Norman and his lawyer were able to do was deny the charges, because there had been no witnesses. Norman was sentenced to six years for molesting, and plotting to abduct across a state border, a minor.

For a while Cathy enjoyed the role of martyr. But she couldn't keep it up more than a few weeks, because it wasn't gay enough. Her legion of boyfriends retreated a little distance, though they still asked her out. As time went on, when Cathy complained about rape, her parents paid not much attention. After all, Cathy had been on The Pill for years now.

Cathy's plans had changed, and she no longer wanted to become a nurse. She was going to be an air hostess. She was sixteen, but could easily pass for twenty or more, if she chose, so she told the airline she was eighteen, and went through their six-week training course in how to turn on the charm, serve drinks and meals graciously to all, soothe the nervous, administer first aid, and carry out emergency exit procedures if necessary. Cathy was a natural at all this. Flying to Rome, Beirut, Teheran, Paris, and having dates all along the way with fascinating men was just her cup of tea. Frequently the air hostesses were supposed to stay overnight in foreign cities, where their hotels were paid for. So life was a breeze. Cathy had money galore, and a collection of the weirdest presents, especially from gentlemen of the Middle East, such as a gold toothbrush and a portable narghile (also of gold) suitable for smoking pot. She had suffered a broken nose, thanks to the insane chauffeur of an Italian millionaire on the cliff-hanging road between Positano and Amalfi. But the nose had been set well, and did not mar her prettiness in the least. To her credit, Cathy sent money regularly to her parents, and she herself had a skyrocketing account in a New York savings bank.

Then the checks to her parents abruptly stopped. The airlines got in touch with Vic and Ruby. Where was Cathy? Vic and Ruby had no idea. She might be anywhere in the world—the Philippines, Hong Kong, even Australia for all they knew. Would the airline please inform them, her parents asked, as soon as they learned anything?

The trail went to Tangiers and ended. Cathy had told another stewardess, it seemed, that she had a big date in Tangiers with a man who was going to pick her up at the airport. Cathy evidently kept that date, and was never heard of again.

The Evangelist

God came late to Diana Redfern—but He came. Diana was forty-two when, walking down her rain-drenched street where droplets fell from the elms, due to a rain which had recently stopped, she experienced a change—a revelation. This revelation involved her mind, body, and also her soul. She realized the presence of nature, and of an all-powerful God streaming through her. At the same moment, the sun which had been forcing its way through the clouds, flooded over her face and body and the whole street, which was called Elm Street.

Diana stood still, her arms outspread, and heedless of what people might think, let her empty shopping bag drop, and knelt on the pavement. Then she arose, and her step became lighter, her chores were done without effort. Suddenly the dinner was ready, her husband Ben and daughter Prunella, aged fourteen, seated at the candlelit table with shrimp cocktails before them.

"Now we shall pray," said Diana, to the surprise of husband and daughter.

They dropped their little shrimp forks, and bowed their heads. There had been something commanding in Diana's voice.

"God is *here*," Diana said in conclusion.

No one could deny that, or deny Diana. Ben gave his daughter a puzzled glance, which was returned by Prunella, then they began eating.

Diana became at once a lay preacher. She started with Tuesday and Thursday afternoon teas at her house, to which she invited neighbors. The neighbors were mostly women, but a few retired men were able to come too. "Are you aware of the constant presence of God?" she would ask. "It is only unlucky people, who have never made acquaintance with God, who could possibly doubt man's immortality, and his eternal life after death."

The neighbors were silent, first because of trying to think of something to reply (the atmosphere was conversational), and then because they really were quite impressed, and preferred to let Diana do the talking. Attendance at her tea parties grew.

Diana began corresponding with elderly people, prisoners, and unwed mothers, whose names she got from her local church. The preacher there was the Reverend Martin Cousins. He approved of Diana's work, and spoke of her from the pulpit as "one among us who is inspired by God."

In the attic which Diana had partly cleared out and now used as her study, she knelt on a small, low stool at dawn every morning for nearly two hours. On Sunday mornings, too early to interfere with churchgoing at 11, she preached from streetcorners, while standing on a Formica chair brought from her kitchen. "I ask not a penny from you. God is not interested in Caesar's coin. I ask that ye give yourselves to God—and kneel." She would hold out her arms, close her eyes, and she inspired quite a few people to kneel. Some people wrote their names and addresses in her big ledger. These people she later wrote to, with the objective of sustaining their faith.

Diana now wore a flowing white robe and sandals, even in the worst weather. She never caught a cold. Diana's eyelids had always been pinkish, as if she needed sleep, but she slept rather a lot, or she had in the past. Now she slept no more than four hours a night in the attic, where she wrote long after midnight. Her lids became pinker, making her eyes appear blue. When she fixed her gaze upon a stranger, he or she was apt to be afraid to move until she had delivered her message, which seemed a personal message: "Only be *aware*—and thou shalt conquer!"

It was hard for Ben to grasp what Diana wanted to achieve. She did not want any helpers, though she worked hard enough to exhaust three or four people. Her behavior caused some embarrassment to Ben, who was manager of a jewelry and watch repair shop in the town of Pawnuk, Minnesota. Pawnuk was a new suburb composed of affluent WASPs who had fled from a nearby metropolis.

"Best to take it easy and be tolerant," thought Ben. "Diana's all on the good side, anyway."

Prunella was somehow frightened of her mother, and stepped aside whenever Diana wanted to pass her in a room or a hall. Even Ben addressed his wife in a deferential manner now, and he sometimes stuttered. Diana was not often at home, however. She had begun making airplane trips to Philadelphia, New York and Boston, the cities most in need of saving, she said. If she had not an auditorium laid on—she was in touch by letter and telephone with various Chambers of Commerce which could arrange these things for her—Diana would walk right into churches and synagogues and take over. In her white robe and sandals whatever the weather, and with her flowing blonde hair, she made a striking figure as she strode down the aisle and mounted the pulpit or took the rostrum. Who could, or dared to, throw her out? She was preaching The Word.

"Brothers—brethren—sisters! Ye must sweep out the cobwebs of the past! Forget the old phrases learnt by heart! Think of yourselves as newborn—as of this hour! Today is your true birthday!"

Though some preachers and rabbis were annoyed, not one ever tried to stop her. All the congregations, like the neighbors Diana addressed on the pavements of her town, kept silent and listened. Within six months, the fame of Diana Redfern had spread all over America. The few who scoffed—and they were very few—kept their criticism mild. Most annoyed were the people of the meat industry, for Diana preached vegetarianism, and her converts were beginning to make a dent in the profits of Chicago's slaughterhouses.

Diana planned a World Tour of Human Resurrection. Money flowed to her, or fell like manna—money from strangers, Frenchmen, Germans, Canadians, people who had only read about her and never seen her. So the expenses of a world tour presented no problem. Some of the money, in fact, Diana sent back to the donors. She was certainly not greedy, but it was soon evident that she could not cope with all her letter writing (more important), if she sent back all the contributions, so she deposited them in a special bank account.

A part-time housekeeper was now preparing the meals for
Diana's household, vegetarian, of course. Often the house resembled a hostel for young and old, because strangers rang the door-
bell, stayed to talk, and Ben had ceased to be surprised by families
with three or more children intending to sleep on the two sofas in
the living room and in the spare bedrooms.

"All, *all* is possible," said Diana to Ben.

Yes, thought Ben. But never had he imagined that his marriage would come to this—Diana isolated from him, sleeping on a
bed of nails, more or less, in the attic, while strangers occupied his
house. He sensed that events were spiraling to a climax with
Diana's round-the-world tour, and that like biblical events they
would be beyond his control. Diana would become something like
a living saint, perhaps, and more famous than any saint alive had
ever been.

The morning of her departure on the world tour, Diana stood
on the sill of her attic window, raised her arms to the rising sun,
and stepped out, convinced that she could fly or at least float. She
fell onto a round, white-painted iron table and the red bricks of
the patio. Thus poor Diana met her earthly end.

The Perfectionist

M argot Fleming's father, whom Margot had greatly admired, had often said to her, "Anything worth doing is worth doing well." Margot believed that anything worth doing well was worth doing perfectly.

The Flemings' house and garden were at all times in perfect order. Margot did all the gardening, though they could have afforded a gardener. Even their Airedale, Rugger, slept only where he was supposed to sleep (on a carpet in front of the fireplace), and never jumped on people to greet them, only wagged his tail. The Flemings' only child, Rosamund, aged fourteen, had perfect manners, and her only fault was that she was inclined to asthma.

If, in putting away a fork in the silverware drawer, Margot noticed an incipient tarnish, she would get out the silver polish and clean the fork, and this would lead, whatever the hour of day or night, to her cleaning the rest of the silverware so it would all look equally nice. Then Margot would be inspired to tackle the tea service, and then the cover for the meat platter, and then there were the silver frames of photographs in the living room, and the silver stamp box on the telephone table, and it might be dawn before Margot was finished. However, there was a housemaid, named Dolly, who came three times a week to do the major cleaning.

Margot seldom dared to prepare a meal for her own family, and never for guests. This, despite a kitchen equipped with every modern convenience, including a walk-in deep freezer, three blending machines, an electric tin-opener and an electric knife-sharpener, a huge stove with two glass-doored ovens in it, and cabinets around the walls full of pressure cookers, colanders, and pots and pans of all sizes. The Flemings almost never ate at home, because Margot was afraid her cooking would not be good enough. Something—maybe the soup, maybe the salad—might not be just right, Margot thought, so she ducked the whole business. The Flemings might ask their friends for drinks before dinner, but then they would all get into their cars and drive eight miles to the city for dinner at a restaurant, then perhaps drive back to the Flemings' for coffee and brandy.

Margot was a bit of a hypochondriac. She got up early every morning (if she was not still up after polishing silver or waxing furniture) to do her Yoga exercises, which were followed by a half hour of meditation. Then Margot weighed herself. If she had lost or gained a fraction of a pound overnight, she would try to remedy this by the way she ate that day. Then she drank the juice of one lemon unsweetened. Twice a year she went for two weeks to a spa, and felt that she got rid of small aches and pains which had started in the preceding six months. At the spa, her diet was even simpler, and her slender face became a little more anxious, though she made an effort to maintain an intelligently pleasant expression, as this was part of the general perfection that she hoped to achieve.

"The So-and-sos are very informal," her husband Harold would say sometimes. "We don't have to give them a banquet, but it would be nice if we could ask them for dinner here." No luck. Margot would say something like:

"I just don't think I can cope with it. A restaurant is so much simpler, Harold dear."

Margot's expression would have become so pained, Harold could never bring himself to argue further. But he often thought, "All that big kitchen, and we can't even ask our friends for an omelet!"

Thus it came as a staggering surprise to Harold when Margot announced one day in October, with the solemnity of a Crusader praying before battle: "Harold, we're going to have a dinner party *here*."

The occasion was a double-barreled one: Harold's birthday was nine days off and fell on a Saturday. And he had just been promoted to vice-president of his bank with a rise in salary. That was enough to warrant a party, and Harold felt he owed it to his colleagues, but still—was Margot capable? "There might be twenty people at least," Harold said. "Even I'd been thinking of a restaurant this time."

But Margot plainly felt it was something she ought to do, to be a perfect wife. She sent out the invitations. She spent two days planning the menu with the aid of *Larousse Gastronomique*, typed it with two carbons, and made a shopping list with two carbons also in case she mislaid one or two of them. This left seven days before the party. She decided that the living room curtains looked faded, so she cruised the city in a taxi looking for the right material, then for just the right gold braid for the edges and the bottom. She made the new curtains herself. She hired an upholsterer to re-cover the sofa and four armchairs, and paid him extra for a rushed job. The already clean windows were washed again by Margot and Dolly, the already clean dinner service (for twenty-four people) washed again also. Margot was up all night the two nights preceding the birthday-promotion party, and of course she was busy during the days, too. She and Dolly made a trial batch of the complicated pudding that was to be the dessert, found it a success, and threw it away.

The big evening came, and twenty-two people arrived between 7:30 and 8 P.M. in a series of private cars and taxis. Margot and a hired butler and Dolly drifted about with trays of drinks and hot canapés and cheese dips. The dining table had been let out to its greatest length—a handsome field of white linen now, silver candelabra, and three vases of red carnations.

And all went well. The women praised the appearance of the table, praised the soup. The men pronounced the claret excellent. The president of Harold's bank proposed a toast to Margot. Then Margot began to feel ill. She had a second coffee, and accepted a second brandy which she didn't want, but one of Harold's senior colleagues had offered it. Then she ducked into her bedroom and took a benzedrine. She was not in the habit of taking pick-up pills, and had these only because she had recently begged her doctor for them "Just in case," and had been given them because she had promised not to abuse them. Ten minutes later, Margot felt up in the air, almost flying, and she became alarmed. She went back to her bedroom and took a mild sleeping pill. She drank another brandy, which someone pressed upon her. Harold proposed another toast, to his bank, and this was followed a few minutes later by a generally proposed toast to Harold, because it was his birthday. Margot dutifully partook of all these toasts. In the last moments of the party, Margot felt she was walking in her sleep, as if she were a ghost, or someone else. When the door closed after the last guest, she collapsed on the floor.

A doctor was summoned. Margot was rushed to hospital, and her stomach pumped. She was unconscious for many hours. "Nothing to worry about, really," the doctor said to Harold. "It's exhaustion plus the fact that her nerves are upset by pills. It's just a matter of flushing out her system." Water was being piped slowly down her throat. Margot regained consciousness, and at once experienced an agony of shame. She was sure she had done something *wrong* at the party, but just what she couldn't remember.

"Margot my dear, you did beautifully!" Harold said. "Everyone said what a superb evening it was!"

But Margot was convinced she had passed out, and that their guests had thought she was drunk. Harold showed Margot appreciative notes he had received from several of their guests, but Margot interpreted them as polite merely.

Once home from the hospital, Margot took to knitting. She had always knitted a little. Now she undertook a vast enterprise: to knit coverlets for every bed in the house (eight counting the twin beds in the two guest rooms). Margot neglected her Yoga meditation, but not her exercises, as she knitted and knitted from 6 A.M. until nearly 2 A.M., hardly pausing to eat.

The doctor told Harold to consult a psychiatrist. The psychiatrist had a chat with Margot, then said to Harold, "We must let her continue knitting, otherwise she may become worse. When she has got all the coverlets done, perhaps we can talk to her."

But Harold suspected that the doctor was only trying to make *him* feel better. Things were worse than ever. Margot stopped Dolly from preparing dinner, saying that Dolly's cooking wasn't good enough. The three Flemings made hurried trips to restaurants, then went back home so Margot could resume her knitting.

Knit, knit, knit. And what will Margot think of to do next?

ABOUT THE AUTHOR

Born in Fort Worth, Texas, in 1921, Patricia Highsmith spent much of her adult life in Switzerland and France. She was educated at Barnard College, where she studied English, Latin, and Greek. Her first novel, *Strangers on a Train*, published initially in 1950, proved to be a major commercial success and was filmed by Alfred Hitchcock. Despite this early recognition, Highsmith was unappreciated in the United States for the entire length of her career.

Writing under the pseudonym of Claire Morgan, she then published *The Price of Salt* in 1953, which had been turned down by her previous American publisher because of its frank exploration of homosexual themes. Her most popular literary creation was Tom Ripley, the dapper sociopath who first debuted in her 1955 novel, *The Talented Mr. Ripley*. She followed with four other Ripley novels. Posthumously made into a major motion picture, *The Talented Mr. Ripley* has helped bring about a renewed appreciation of Highsmith's work in the United States as has the posthumous publication of *The Selected Stories*, which received widespread acclaim when it was published by W. W. Norton & Company in 2001.

The author of more than twenty books, Highsmith has won the O. Henry Memorial Award, the Edgar Allan Poe Award, Le Grand Prix de Littérature Policière, and the Award of the Crime Writers' Association of Great Britain. She died in Switzerland on February 4, 1995, and her literary archives are maintained in Berne.